SHE DIED BECAUSE...

KENNETH HOPKINS

Also available in Perennial Library by
Kenneth Hopkins:
DEAD AGAINST MY PRINCIPLES

SHE DIED BECAUSE...

KENNETH HOPKINS

PERENNIAL LIBRARY
Harper & Row, Publishers
New York, Cambridge, Philadelphia, San Francisco
London, Mexico City, São Paulo, Sydney

SHE DIED BECAUSE ... Copyright © 1957 by Kenneth Hopkins. All rights reserved. Printed in the United States of America. No part of this book may be used or reproduced in any manner whatsoever without written permission except in the case of brief quotations embodied in critical articles and reviews. For information address Holt, Rinehart & Winston, 521 Fifth Avenue, New York, N.Y. 10175.

First PERENNIAL LIBRARY edition published 1984.

Library of Congress Cataloging in Publication Data

Hopkins, Kenneth.
  She died because ...

  "Perennial Library."
  Originally published: Holt, Rinehart and Winston, 1957.
  I. Title.
PR6015.062S5 1984b   823'.914   83-48952
ISBN 0-06-080718-0 (pbk.)

84 85 86 87 88 10 9 8 7 6 5 4 3 2 1

To E. H. Visiak,

as dedicated a scholar as

Dr. Blow, but luckier with

his domestics.

"This Essay, such as it is, was
thought by some, who knew of it,
not amiss to be published; that
so many things remarkable, dispers'd
before, now brought under one view,
might not hazard to be otherwise
lost, nor the labour lost of
collecting them."

—JOHN MILTON
A Brief History of Muscovia

SHE DIED BECAUSE...

1

Dr. William Blow moved uneasily in his chair and a small frown appeared, deepening the already deep lines of his brow. He laid down his pen.

Dr. Blow didn't yet understand the cause of his own distress. His mind was still mainly occupied with the problems of editing the text of the whole works of Samuel Butler, a task upon which he had now been engaged for some fifteen years—ever since he completed his monumental edition of the whole works of Abraham Cowley.

But something must have interrupted his train of thought . . . and he set himself to discover what it was. Some disturbance in the street, perhaps? But there, all was still. In the house? In the room itself? No, seemingly not. Some distraction arising from the text before him? Much more likely! He applied his thoughts again to the lines he had been about to annotate:

> And he's approv'd the most deserving
> Who longest can hold out at starving . . .

That was it!

Dr. Blow was hungry.

Strange, that, for he never was hungry before that he could remember. It was, indeed, one of his reasons for employing a housekeeper. Mrs. Sollihull's duties included the preparation and serving of meals. His breakfast at ten, his lunch at one-thirty, his tea at five, his dinner at a quarter to eight precisely, and his little bit of supper on a tray soon after ten, ready for him to eat at about midnight if he felt so inclined. There was certainly no tray in the room now, so it could not yet be ten o'clock. Had he, then, dined? Had he, in fact, had his afternoon tea? That at least was easily established, for today was Tuesday, the day he had muffins; and of course the most careful consumer of muffins must leave, here and there, a little grease on his manuscript. It didn't at all matter, for naturally everything had to be rewritten many times before being sent to the press; and the stains in any case could hardly—ha! ha!—communicate themselves to the printed book. No. . . .

There seemed not to be any recent traces of muffin. On the other hand, it was quite dark. True, the evenings drew in—or were they drawing out just now? He could never really master that little problem. But it would hardly be dark before tea. It must be quite dark now, because he had the table light on, its little pool of radiance falling on the books and papers before him but leaving the corners of the room in shadow, for the big center light was off.

Dr. Blow rose to his feet. If it were Tuesday, it could hardly be Mrs. Sollihull's afternoon off; for that came on Wednesday. On the other hand, if he hadn't had muffins, perhaps it was Wednesday! And yet he had always taken meals on Wednesdays in the past. There was some long-standing arrangement about it.

He moved to the door, opened it, and stood a moment listening. No sound, no light either, except the faint glow behind him from the reading lamp. He switched on the hall light and went along to the kitchen. Mrs. Sollihull wasn't there, and the fire was out. The kitchen clock said twenty to three, which was absurd. Why, if it were twenty to three he would barely have finished his lunch; he would at all events not be hungry.

He now visited every room in turn, taking them as they came, first the bathroom, then the spare back bedroom, then his own bedroom, then the drawing room, then the dining room, and then his study. Only the housekeeper's room remained, and at this door he hesitated. It was ten years and more since he had been in that room. He'd not so much as looked through the open door, so far as he could remember, since the time of Mrs. Hoptroft, that dreadful woman. Mrs. Hoptroft had once called "come in" when he tapped, and when he entered, he had found her quite unclothed and laughing at him. A pity, for he had never since had a housekeeper—and he'd had many—with quite Mrs. Hoptroft's touch with toasted cheese.

So he hesitated at Mrs. Sollihull's door (formerly Mrs. Hoptroft's) and then, tentatively, he knocked.

"Mrs. Sollihull!" he called softly.

He heard nothing but the distant, ever-present murmur of the sea.

"Mrs. Sollihull!"—louder—and at the same time he slowly turned the door handle. The door opened with a small swish against the pile of the fitted carpet. This room, like the others, was in darkness. Dr. Blow didn't care, yet, to venture in. A man might in emergency open his housekeeper's door. But it was hardly his business to enter, especially if she were not there. And she seemed not to be there. At least, she made no answer.

Of course, she might be sleeping, if it were Wednesday, her afternoon out. A woman sometimes likes to lie down, he believed. He would not switch on the light. He would go back and put on the main light in his study, opposite. This, with the dimmer light of the hall already burning, would afford sufficient illumination for him to see into Mrs. Sollihull's room without awakening her if she were asleep. He congratulated himself on this diplomatic solution and at once put it into effect. The study light blazed out and threw a strong glow through Mrs. Sollihull's open door, revealing Mrs. Sollihull lying on the carpet by the fireplace.

"Just so," said Dr. Blow. "Exactly. It must be Wednesday." He closed the door softly, and paused. But—as he had already reflected—even on Wednesday he was entitled to eat. Unless, indeed, he had forgotten to go to tea with somebody. It wouldn't be with Willis, for Willis was in South Africa now. A nice fellow, Willis; he missed him.

No, not Willis. Not Mrs. Maggs, because she always sent her car to collect him. Not Forrest, for he never asked him to tea, only to lunch, and by twenty to three (a quarter to, now) lunch would be over and (he reminded himself, almost desperately) if lunch was over, why was he hungry?

Well, of course, it must be Manciple who was expecting him! Manciple, always vague about these things, was probably expecting him to tea, and had in fact forgotten to ask him! Should he go down at once or telephone him up and pull his leg gently first? Telephone, perhaps; because it remained just possible that Manciple had, in fact, not forgotten to ask him, but had not intended to do so. All the same, no doubt he would give him tea in this emergency. And it was an emergency. Stupid, to go through the best part of the afternoon, and doubtless the whole morning, thinking it was Tuesday!

He returned to the study and closed the door. His conversation would in no sense be private, but he considered that the use of the telephone, at all times a tricky business, was better conducted in seclusion. Very deliberately he dialed Manciple's number, which was written on a piece of paper pinned above the telephone. On the paper were all the telephone numbers Dr. Blow ever used, about nine of them; they were those of the London Library, of his club in London, of the railway station and a taxi stand, of Cakebread's Domestic Agency, of his doctor, and of a couple of local friends, of whom Professor Manciple (who lived in the flat below) was in every sense the nearest.

Dr. Blow heard the buzz-buzz which he knew meant that the connection was made, and then the lifting of his neighbor's instrument which was the preliminary to conversation. As with many elderly persons, this to him was victory.

"Hullo, is that you, Manciple?" he shouted, as though his friend were in New York. "Manciple, my dear fellow, are you expecting me to tea?"

Professor Manciple in the flat below pulled his dressing gown irritably about him and answered as patiently as he could, "Blow, what makes you think it's teatime?"

"I'm hungry," said Dr. Blow.

"Go and cut yourself a lump of bread, then. Every time you're hungry doesn't mean it's teatime. I've been in bed the best part of an hour. It's just on three."

"Three, just so! But do you mean three in the morning? Then that explains why the fire is out. Manciple, Mrs. Sollihull is lying there on the carpet; I looked in—just peeped, you know, after knocking. She ought to be in bed. Is it Wednesday?"

"The day makes no difference, Blow. It's the middle of the night, that's what matters. I was nearly asleep. No doubt Mrs. Sollihull *is* asleep, lucky woman. If I asked you to tea yesterday, which I didn't, you're too late. And if I asked you for today, which I haven't, you're too early."

"But it means I haven't had my dinner, then. No wonder I'm hungry. Why didn't she call me?"

"She probably called you till she was blue in the face. You know you never take any notice. Some damned footnote bothering you or something. I say, are you sure she's lying on the carpet?"

"Oh, yes, quite sure—with her mouth open."

"Well, wait where you are and I'll come up and help you to cut a sandwich, and then we'll see. I don't think she ought to be lying on the carpet."

"She's in her own room, you know."

"Wait." The Professor rang off, and Dr. Blow put his own receiver back on the hook. A sandwich would be something, but —he wondered—ought it to be sweet, as for tea, or savory, as for dinner? He went out into the hall, ready to let Professor Manciple in when he rang. He didn't open the flat door because of standing in a draft, but when the shadow of Manciple appeared against the glass he at once let him in.

"Don't ring the bell, my dear fellow," he called. "I can see you!"

Professor Manciple was still in pajamas and dressing gown, but over this he wore his overcoat, and he had a pair of galoshes over his slippers.

"Now I'm here," he said, "put the kettle on and we'll have a cup of tea."

"Ah, yes," said Blow, "I feel sure I missed my tea." He led the way to the kitchen.

The two men spoke little at first. Blow put the kettle on and got out cups and plates. Manciple cut bread and butter and found a few slices of ham and some bananas. He felt a bit peckish himself now he was broad awake.

At last, as he poured boiling water into the teapot, Blow

said over his shoulder, "I've put in an extra spoonful. I suppose Mrs. Sollihull will want a cup if we wake her."

"Let's go along while it's brewing," Manciple suggested.

They went quietly along to the housekeeper's room and Blow discreetly tapped on the door.

There was no reply.

"I think, as you are with me, I feel justified in going right in," Dr. Blow whispered. "You must be prepared to be a witness that I did nothing improper." He opened the door and switched on the light. "There she is," he said triumphantly.

Mrs. Sollihull still lay on the carpet with her mouth open. Her eyes were open, too. But she never moved.

"If you ask me," Professor Manciple said from his position half in and half out of the door, "the woman's dead."

"Nonsense," Blow replied. "She can't be more than fifty. She's in the prime of life. Of course she isn't dead; she's walking in her sleep, only, of course, she isn't actually walking." And he shook her by the shoulder. "Wake up, Mrs. Sollihull!"

Mrs. Sollihull sagged a little.

"Besides, what did she die of, then?" asked Dr. Blow, his voice a shade less confident.

Manciple craned his head farther into the room to get a clearer view.

"I'm half-inclined to think," he said, "that she's got a knife in her back."

2

"Tch!" said Dr. Blow.

The two old gentlemen were back in the kitchen facing one another over cups of tea laced with brandy. Professor Manciple dipped a Garibaldi biscuit into his cup and said nothing.

"Really," the Doctor went on, "a man might almost as well enter into matrimony these days. Housekeepers are a constant source of annoyance. I've had to speak to Mrs. Sollihull more than once, and she has been here scarcely a fortnight. And now this. Her references were impeccable—I use the word somewhat loosely, I know; but I'm upset. I say, this is awfully good ham, Manciple."

"I think, Blow, we must telephone to the police."

"Do you think we must? There's quite a civil constable I see sometimes passing at the corner. He would probably come in if we could catch him. But I'm really very doubtful if I have their telephone number, and, you know, it's four o'clock in the morning. I wouldn't hesitate if Mrs. Sollihull were breathing, but we did satisfy ourselves. What can the police do?"

"My dear fellow, you must really try to be a little practical. It is a misfortune if one's housekeeper dies, of course it is; but to neglect proper steps thereafter is possibly actively criminal. Sudden death is always the concern of the police, and if you address an inquiry to the telephone supervisor, he will connect you with them at once. It's his business, Blow; the fellow sits there all night waiting for people to call him up. So do the police. They get time off next day. They'll be glad to hear from you probably. Come now!"

17

"I must have a witness, then. You'll stay, Manciple? 'He that with injury is griev'd, and goes to law to be reliev'd, is sillier than a sottish chouse. . . .' Well, come into the study, then."

In the study Dr. Blow felt a little easier; it was home. Whereas he never felt wholly comfortable in the kitchen. The reading lamp still cast its warm glow on the books and papers that littered the writing table; and now that the center light was on, too, the rows of books round the walls shone in their polished leather and gold. The Doctor made his way once again to the telephone, and without undue hesitation dialed a number.

"If you're telephoning me," Professor Manciple observed, "you can spare yourself the labor. I'm here."

Dr. Blow hung up and laughed in his high, cracked voice. "I must really remember to tell that to Whitgift," he said. "I telephoned up Manciple, I shall tell him, and all the time Manciple was standing at my elbow! Why was I telephoning you, my dear fellow?"

"You're supposed to be telephoning the police."

"Ah, yes. I must dial O. 'All things say O to him,' as Man Friday puts it. We must never despise Defoe, eh? Oh. Could you, I wonder, connect me with the police station. I am unable to give you the number, but perhaps you have it at the telephone exchange. An extraordinary thing has happened here; my housekeeper . . ."

"Don't!" cried the Professor.

Dr. Blow looked surprised, and fell silent.

"Most improper to tell the telephone operator before you tell the police," Manciple went on. "Police work is confidential, you know."

"Ah. Is that the police station? Just so. I am telephoning up about my housekeeper, Mrs. Sollihull. Sollihull—certainly not, my name is Blow: BLOW, Blow, Dr. Blow. I must explain that I am not, however, a Doctor of Medicine. I should, in that event, have known at once that she was dead; as it was, Manciple told me. Manciple. Dear me, he is internationally known, I assure you. I must ask you not to interrupt. My housekeeper, Mrs. Sollihull, when she didn't bring my tea, you understand, as she always does, or rather did—at first I thought it was Wednesday, which would have explained it. Yes, you foolish fellow, I know it is Wednesday now, but it wasn't yesterday. Really, the police are too stupid—he's saying now, Manciple, that it *is* Wednesday. . . . Policeman! You must please listen carefully or call one of your superiors. I am being very patient with you. My house-keeper, Mrs. Sollihull, is lying dead in her room. I have a witness. Now, I want you to come round here first thing in the morning and deal with it—what time do you open? There is the body and everything. I shall be obliged to go out to breakfast in the circumstances, but I shall return by ten o'clock. Oh, certainly, if you prefer it. The address is Ten Priory Place; it is the second turning on the left after you pass the junction of North Street with High Street; and we are at the lower end, overlooking the sea—number ten, the top flat. I shall be waiting for you. It is very early, but you know your own business best. Good-bye."

Once again the telephone was carefully replaced on its hook, and the Doctor turned to his friend.

"You will have heard the gist of that," he said. "The police are coming at once. An extraordinary fellow, that was. Polite, I concede, but very unwilling to allow me to say anything. Well, we must wait now."

"I think, as the woman was your housekeeper and I hardly knew her, it will not be improper for me to smoke a cigarette," Manciple said.

"And I will join you," said Dr. Blow. "It is a foolish prejudice to suggest that a proper respect on these occasions enjoins ab-stinence from any suitable activity. A cigarette will certainly steady our nerves. And the nerves are a vital part of the system; it is no less legitimate than it would be to take a little stimulant for the heart; and—the thought occurs—why not a little stim-ulant also? I believe it is customary to offer something to the police. Not gin, I think, but brandy is quite a dignified drink. Let us take a glass each."

"Blow," the Professor began slowly, as they sat nursing their glasses, "does it seem likely to you that there has been foul play? Surely nobody, least of all one's housekeeper, gets stabbed in the back by accident. Forgive me, my dear fellow—we're old friends —there was nothing, was there, in the way of horseplay between you?"

"Horseplay, Manciple? I hardly knew the woman. Horseplay! Come, come. I have been busy all day with my notes. It wasn't even her afternoon out—I mean, supposing horseplay, as you term it, to have been among her indulgences. It is certainly not among mine. I don't say it was an accident and I don't say it wasn't. All I say is Mrs. Sollihull had no business to be involved in matters of this sort, whatever their ostensible nature. There are standards of behavior and conduct—I distinguish between the two, making the one general in application and the other moral—which domestics must be prepared to observe, especially senior domestics. The woman would have had to go."

"I never really thought . . . , but it struck me, perhaps, that while you were showing her—complaining, possibly—how the knife had not been properly washed up, let us say, it might have slipped."

"But not into her back, Manciple; unless, indeed, I had been trying to attract attention from eyes in the back of her head. No, no! I never interfere in the washing-up; the knives are spotless, I assure you. And I think she brought the knife with her. From what I could see, it didn't look like one of my grandmother's. I have all her cutlery, and napery, too, for that matter. I say, did I tell them to ring the top bell at number ten or number twelve, do you remember; I sometimes say number twelve, you know, when I mean number ten; because I always remember that you are number ten and I look upon you as next door, although it is not quite that when you are one floor below. If they rouse up that woman in the colored woolens and the beads, it will be dreadful. She will rouse the whole street with her cries. We had better go down and intercept them."

"Can't you flash a light from the window?"

"Better not. I think the minimum of activity of all kinds is to be desired. Let us creep down in stocking feet and meet them at the corner."

Accordingly, they made their way cautiously down to street

level and looked at the right and to the left. There wasn't a soul in sight. Deep in conversation, but with voices decently subdued, they strolled toward the sea front just below the house. The first light of dawn flushed the waters moving in their priestlike task. Dr. Blow drank in the poetry of the scene.

"There go the ships," he said, waving a hand at the empty horizon, "and there is that Leviathan. But Hobbes, of course, was not a fisherman. I often wonder how he came to borrow the word from the deep to signify despotic power."

"To Hobbes, as perhaps to Milton, and certainly later to Descartes—Berkeley, too . . . ," the Professor began, carefully marshaling thoughts neither uncomplicated nor concise; but Blow interrupted.

"Isn't that a policeman?" he said excitedly, and without waiting for an answer he began hurrying back. "Don't ring the bell at number twelve!" he cried in his high-pitched voice, "we don't want a disturbance!"

A police sergeant and a constable stood at the front door.

"I am Sergeant Wix, sir."

"Just so. This is Professor Gideon Manciple and I am Dr. Blow. You must come in, Sergeant. We were just beginning a most interesting discussion about Hobbes—*Leviathan,* you know. Come upstairs, but please don't make unnecessary noise. You may perhaps think fit to take your boots off. I am always careful not to disturb the people in the other flats, especially Commander Egan on the first floor. He bangs on his ceiling, which is Professor Manciple's floor, on the slightest provocation. A real man of war, ha ha—retired, of course, but very active. Here we are, come in. The stairs are a trial to strangers, but I shall offer you a rather choice Armagnac—it's the Kressmann—a really astonishing spirit for the money."

"Where is the body, sir?"

"Oh, in her room, of course. I shall show you presently. But undoubtedly dead, Sergeant. There can be no pressing hurry. You must be patient while the Professor and I get our breath; we are not so agile as you younger men, and I for one have been a good deal agitated, though I am calmer now. You must know that Mrs. Sollihull only came to me about a fortnight ago from Cakebread's Agency. Cakebread's are usually reliable."

"We like to look at the body first, as a rule, sir."

"So you shall, Sergeant, so you shall. Let me see, I think perhaps, Manciple, if you would help me with the feet we could bring it into the kitchen, where it's warmer. Mrs. Sollihull's room strikes quite chilly."

"*In situ,* sir, if you please. Will you show the way?"

"Come along, then, come along. Manciple, you must come, too. You are a witness. Come, gentlemen!"

This time Dr. Blow felt justified in putting on the light in the housekeeper's room. He pressed the switch, and a bright light shone exactly over the middle of the carpet where the body lay. The Doctor and the Professor stood aside just within the room, and the two policemen advanced, keeping carefully clear of the body itself. They stood one on each side, looking down. And then they looked at one another.

"Flash Elsie!" said Sergeant Wix.

3

"May we go back to your study now, sir?"

"Back? Yes, of course. But don't you take fingerprints and collect clues? Masterman, you know, Manciple, writes detective fiction. I read something of it. Clues is the word for what one might call the *apparatus critica*."

"All that will be attended to, sir. For the present we will let things alone and retire, if you please. I may be frank with you gentlemen. My instructions are to ascertain the immediate facts. Your phone call was thought a little confused, if you will excuse my saying so. Indeed it comes rather as a surprise to me to find a body at all. In the majority of cases involving housekeepers the lady has disappeared with the silver."

"Dear me, there was no suggestion of that. In fact, she didn't even use one of my own knives, eh—er, where *is* the knife?"

Using one hand only, and keeping well away so as to disturb nothing, the constable slightly raised the body. Nothing lay beneath it.

"Stabbed, all right, Sarge," he said, stepping back, "but no weapon."

"It was there," Manciple affirmed. "We saw it."

"Sticking out of her back," Blow agreed. "It was that that made us suspicious. But it definitely wasn't one of grandmother's."

"Well, where is it?" asked the Sergeant.

Nobody answered.

Sergeant Wix moved over to the windows and looked out, pulling back the heavy curtains. He looked across to the backs of the houses in the next street. He noticed that both windows were fastened with heavy, old-fashioned catches. He dropped the curtains and came back to the door.

"I shall lock this door and retain the key, if you please. And I must ask to use your telephone. Then you shall make statements, gentlemen. Elkins, you take a look round the flat and then stay where you can see this door. I don't want to lose the body, too. Now, gentlemen."

The three of them returned to the study, and Wix telephoned the police station. Blow and Manciple sat rather glumly, one on each side of the fireplace.

"Wix here. Get me through to Inspector Urry, will you?"

"I used to know an Urry," said Dr. Blow. "Poor fellow."

"Inspector? Wix here, sir. I'm at Ten Priory Place, top flat, name of Blow. Housekeeper dead, sir. Stabbed. Yes, sir. Yes. Yes. Yes, sir. Right."

"He seems to get on well enough with his superiors," Blow observed.

The Sergeant had rung off now.

"I'm to get preliminary statements from you, sir. The Inspector will be here shortly. Will you excuse me, Professor? I must see Dr. Blow alone—and you afterward. You might feel you would like to go along to the kitchen where it's warm, as Dr. Blow pointed out a while ago. But please don't leave the flat."

"I think I will fry myself an egg, Blow."

"Fry one for me, Manciple. And for the Sergeant?"

"Thank you sir, no. Now, if I may. Your name? Age? Occupation?"

"Blow, BLOW, Blow, Dr. William. Oh, seventy-odd. It's in *Who's Who*—I really forget. I'm a scholar."

"A scholar, sir?"

"A scholar, you know. An author, if you like. I'm annotating Butler. Zachary Grey's work is of course invaluable, but two centuries cannot pass without the need for something more; and I find Russel Nash far from wholly satisfactory. Waller's Butler is, of course—well, Waller, you know. . . ."

"Are any of these gentlemen directly involved in our present

24

inquiry, sir? Because if not, may I ask you to tell me exactly what occurred before you telephoned the police?"

"Goodness, they're all dead, Sergeant, all dead. But not murdered, I trust. Ha ha, not murdered. Hem. Well, you see, I was working here at my desk—there are my notes and books as I left them: the first edition of 1663; Grey's two volumes, with the Hogarth plates; Nash; Waller, too. And, of course, Thyer and others. Yes. I have everything at my elbow, it's the only way. That's why I would never annotate Voltaire, although his points of similarity with Butler in certain moods must be admitted to be of wide interest. Yes. . . . There's no need for you to write all this down, my dear fellow. I've already developed it in a paper read to the Royal Society of Literature; it's in the *Transactions*. You are insensibly leading me on to talk shop, I fear. . . . Well, I was working, and I began to feel hungry. I looked for Mrs. Sollihull to ask her if she had forgotten my tea, because even if it is her afternoon off—I always give them an afternoon every week, you know. It is necessary for health; and, indeed, they demand it—what was I saying? Ah yes, my tea was late. Well, I telephoned up Manciple—he lives next door, you know. We go to tea with one another sometimes. But he wasn't expecting me to tea yesterday, because, foolishly, I thought it was yesterday, you know. Or Wednesday, one or the other. It made quite a difference because of Mrs. Sollihull's day off, which would have been Wednesday, poor woman, today. And I didn't like to go in without a witness. So there she was, and we had a cup of tea, Manciple and I, that is, and telephoned up for you. That's all."

"You looked into her room, and saw her?"

"I looked in; she seemed to be asleep. Then Manciple said she wouldn't go to sleep on the carpet like that. Well, I didn't know; I never went into her room before, not since Mrs. Hoptroft. When Manciple came we went in together and he said, 'Look, she's got a knife in her back,' or something like that. And she had. You could see it sticking out."

"After you telephoned, you left the flat together?"

"Yes. We thought we'd better meet you instead of waiting until you rang the bell, in case you rang the wrong bell."

"You left the flat open?"

"Unlocked, certainly, because otherwise, unless I'd taken my key, which I sometimes forget to do, we'd have had to rouse Mrs. Sollihull to let us in again, and that would have been useless in the circumstances. It was because she was dead that we had gone out at all."

"How long had Mrs. Sollihull been with you?"

"About two weeks, from Cakebread's. They know me. I must have a sober, God-fearing woman. I am not afraid of God myself, but it is most desirable in domestics. Middle-aged or elderly, of course. One can't have followers. Marriage, of course, is admirable, but not in housekeepers."

"She was a satisfactory housekeeper?"

"Well, I had to speak to her once or twice. But this is the first real cause for dissatisfaction that she has given."

"And the last, sir."

"Exactly. So it is. That reminds me, I must telephone up Cakebread's."

"Later, sir, if you don't mind. And they won't be at the office at six in the morning. Now, what about Mrs. Sollihull's next of kin?"

"I really can't say. I believe she once received a picture postcard by the morning delivery. But I made no inquiry into her affairs."

"She brought her cards, of course?"

"Cards? A Tarot pack do you mean, or what, pray?"

"Insurance cards, for stamping."

"Oh, all that business I leave to them. They buy everything out of the housekeeping, stamps and that. Insurances are paid by banker's order. Then there's my solicitors. I never bother with anything but my work. Except that I insist on buying my own footwear—most important, that. Feet, my father used to say, are at the bottom of everything. He was one of the original contributors to *Punch* under Douglas Jerrold."

"Now I must ask you, sir, if you consider Professor Manciple *quite reliable*. This is in confidence."

"My dear fellow, Manciple is the final authority. Reliable,

say you? He is infallible. He annihilated Pabst, I can assure you."

"You don't think he also annihilated Mrs. Sollihull?"

"Certainly not. She was in no sense a student of numismatics, except—ha ha—on Friday mornings. Pay day, you know! Ha!"

"Well, sir, that seems to be all for the present. I shall get this copied for you to sign formally later. And, of course, the Inspector will wish to go over it again in greater detail. And now I will have a word with Professor Manciple, if he has eaten his egg. May I speak to him in here?"

At this juncture Manciple appeared, carrying a tray. "Eggs for two," he said cheerfully. "And coffee. Come, Sergeant, don't be bashful. Your colleague isn't. He's eaten a quite remarkable quantity of buttered toast. Blow, you go out into the kitchen; I've left yours on the hob. I'll have mine here with the Sergeant. He won't be able to ask so many questions with his mouth full."

The Doctor accordingly departed to the kitchen, the original hunger that had aroused him from his labors those several hours ago returning with full force, despite the ham and bananas.

On the hob, sure enough, was a plate of eggs, a rack of toast, a pot of coffee. On the floor in front of the fire lay the body of Police-Constable Elkins.

"Oh, really!" said Dr. Blow. "Well, this time it can wait." And he drew up a chair and fell to.

The Doctor ate slowly, but less slowly than usual, and indeed a little uneasily, because he had nothing to read. It interested him after thirty years or so in the flat to discover at last why he was never really comfortable in the kitchen; of course, there were no books in it. As he ate his toast he amused himself by translating the gas-meter record card into Greek, but it was a poor diversion. He sighed as he finished, and wondered if he wouldn't have had better sport with Hebrew.

"They must have finished by now," he reflected, "unless Manciple is talking shop again. Let him get started on George III ha'pennies. . . . Well! I'll go and see."

As he drew level with the front door a shadow darkened the glass. "Don't ring," he called, "I can see you!" On the threshold outside stood three tall men in macintoshes.

"Inspector Urry, sir," said the tallest. "Are you Dr. Blow? May we come in? Sergeant Elgar and Detective-Constable Temple, these are. I'm afraid you'll be seeing a good deal of us for a day or two, if what they tell me is true. Lost your housekeeper, haven't you?"

"Dear me, I hope not. We locked her in. Well, come along. I'll take you to the study. Urry. I wonder if you are related to the Urry I knew as a boy: Urry of Merton. Manciple, you remember old Looksharp, don't you? Came in last in the 440 yards."

"Ah, Wix," said the Inspector, ignoring all this. "There you are."

"I've got the statements, sir. Straightforward enough. Will you look at the body first; then we can get it away?"

"Yes. Elgar, call in the photographer. Temple, fingerprints. Where's Elkins? Didn't he come with you, Wix?"

"I think he's in the kitchen," said Dr. Blow, mildly.

"Now, sir," said Wix, producing the door key. The procession moved across the passage and Wix solemnly threw open the door. "The Body, sir," he said with some ceremony.

"Very nice," Inspector Urry answered. But he stayed on the edge of the room, looking in, taking in every detail: the drawn curtains, the undisturbed bed, the quiet corpse. Then he took one step forward, and stopped.

"Flash Elsie!" said Inspector Urry.

"Just so, sir," said Sergeant Wix, with a smirk. "So that's where she got to."

Dr. Blow edged forward. "Isn't it Mrs. Sollihull?" he asked anxiously. "I am really not prepared for any more shocks."

"That's as may be, sir. I can't say fairer than that."

"At all events, you might be a bit clearer," Manciple put in. "Dr. Blow is very naturally concerned. It is he who has lost a housekeeper, after all."

Dr. Blow looked at his watch. But before the conversation could continue, the party was interrupted by a loud voice on the stairs.

"Blow! Blow! Are you giving a party? D'ye know it's barely

six, hey? Get those cars out of the street! No parking, sir, d'ye hear? Street's a bedlam. Hey?"

Blow called peaceably down the stairwell. "It is really all in order, Commander. Police, you know. A little formality, a small matter of entirely confidential private business, my dear Egan. In no sense a maritime preoccupation; entirely civil, I assure you. The cars are not technically parked, you know. Just setting down and taking up. Don't disturb yourself, pray."

"Disturb myself! No need to with you trampling about and doing it for me! What are you up to, Blow? Bless me, Manciple, too! Is the whole house gone mad?"

The Commander had been mounting the stairs all this time and now appeared in the flat itself. He was a very small man, with angry eyes and hardly any hair. He strode forward importantly and came to a halt before the housekeeper's body.

"What's been happening to Mrs. Sollihull?" he demanded.

"Well, thank goodness somebody knows her," said Dr. Blow.

"You identify this cadaver, sir?" said Sergeant Wix.

The Commander stared at him. "Identify her? Certainly. Everyone knows Mrs. Sollihull. Blow's housekeeper. I've known her for years."

"For years, sir? How interesting. Dr. Blow says she's only been in his service a fortnight."

4

"Eh?" said the Commander.

"A fortnight."

"Well, all I can say is, she's remarkably like the last one. Goes clumping down the stairs every morning with a shopping basket."

"The shopping basket belongs to the house," Dr. Blow said mildly, "if you identify her by that."

Here, Inspector Urry interposed. "Come, gentlemen, this is not the moment for trivialities. The housekeeper is dead; we'll go into her shopping habits in the course of our investigation, but not now, please. Not now. Thank you, Commander, for your help. I won't keep you. Thank you, Professor Manciple, you'll be hearing from us. Now, sir, my men must get to their work here. Shall we return to your study."

Under this direct attack the circle broke up. Manciple backed out into the hall and Commander Egan followed. The Doctor led Urry to the study. The policemen moved about their several tasks, and then, without warning, there came a piercing howl from the kitchen and a tall bony woman in woolens, with streaming hair and wild eyes, burst into the study.

"There's a copper dead in the kitchen!" she cried, and slid in a swoon at the Inspector's feet.

"Is there!" said the Inspector, grimly. "Then I'll know the reason why!" He hurried into the hall and bumped into Sergeant Wix, white-faced.

"It's Elkins, all right. Lying on the floor. Poison, I suspect." He threw a sharp glance at Professor Manciple.

"Poison is a woman's weapon," Dr. Blow remarked wisely.

"In any case, I have an alibi." Now that it was morning he felt wide awake and was taking a great interest in this novel experience. It must be all of twenty years since so many as eight people had been in his flat at one time. True, two of them were dead, but even so it represented quite an influx, quite, one might almost say, a prolixity of persons. It served to save one from getting stale.

The unfortunate constable was removed from the flat on a stretcher much more expeditiously than Mrs. Sollihull was. There was no measuring, no taking of fingerprints, not even any photographing. From the study Manciple and Blow merely heard a certain shuffling and heavy breathing as the ambulance men left, and that was all. Really, Blow told himself, one might suppose they were being robbed of constables every day.

"Now!" said Inspector Urry briskly, as he returned. "Where were we?"

"There's that woman, sir," Sergeant Wix reminded him. "The one that squeaked out."

The lady lay on the floor where she had fallen, neither Blow nor Manciple having cared to interfere—indeed, they had drifted into a conversation about the influence of Jocelin of Brakelond on Thomas Carlyle and had forgotten her.

"Ah, yes. Well, give me a cup of water and we'll see what we can do."

"I have heard that they light a piece of brown paper under the nose," Dr. Blow observed.

But before this or any remedy could be applied, the lady suddenly sat up.

"Ah, madam," said the Inspector, pleasantly, "you have had a shock, I fear. But it's all over now. What is your name, please? And would you tell us why you were in Dr. Blow's kitchen? And what you saw there, apart from the constable who was taken ill?"

"Dead, he was. You hold a mirror to their lips and it goes cloudy if they're breathing. I held a saucepan lid. He was dead. My name is Ellen Fisk, Miss Ellen Fisk. The minister will speak for me. And all I wanted was a pinch of ground almonds. The front door was open, so I came in. 'Got a pinch of ground almonds, love?' I said to Mrs. Sollihull—she knows I'd do the same for her anytime—but then I saw she wasn't there and there was only this policeman. So I knelt down with the saucepan lid, and he was dead. So I shouted out, the same as anybody would."

"Where do you live, Miss Fisk?"

"I'm the top flat of number twelve."

"Yes, that is true," Blow put in. "I very often hear her singing through the wall."

"Singing through the wall?"

"Through the wall, singing. Dear me, how pedantic you policemen are."

"I have one of the finest untrained contralto voices St. Bede's mixed choir ever had, the choirmaster always says."

"If you live at number twelve, Miss Fisk, at the top, and this is number ten, at the top, don't you feel it was a long way to come for a pinch of ground almonds? Have you no nearer neighbors?"

"Well, I nip over the chimneys, you know. It's as near as any."

"Over the chimneys?"

"There's an iron fire escape leading up onto the roof; and an agile person can creep along the full length of the street, if he so desires, by the different leads. A passage was marked out during the war, I believe, to admit of access to burning incendiary bombs, and I suppose also as a possible means of escape." As he gave this supplementary information, Dr. Blow looked at Miss Fisk with undisguised distaste.

The lady was wearing a long skirt of some heavy flowered material and a scarlet woolen pullover under a woolen jacket, worked in small, multicolored squares like a bedspread. A necklace made apparently of walnut shells hung round her neck and clicked an accompaniment when she spoke. On her head she wore what might have passed for a nightcap, if it had not rather obviously been a striped football stocking cut down. She was still sitting on the floor.

"You knew Mrs. Sollihull well, Miss Fisk? It was quite customary to borrow items of household utility from her?"

"Well, only ground almonds, naturally. I wouldn't dream of asking for marmalade or thin Captain biscuits. Mrs. Sollihull understood. She was quite the lady."

"Did Mrs. Sollihull ever climb over the roofs to borrow anything?"

"Oh, no, that was never Mrs. Sollihull's way."

"You just came straight in and went along to the kitchen?"

"That's right."

"Then how do you know Mrs. Sollihull is dead?"

"I told you, it was a policeman. Mrs. Sollihull wasn't there."

"But she's dead, Miss Fisk. Murdered, Miss Fisk. Now, Miss Fisk: WHAT WERE YOU IN DR. BLOW'S KITCHEN FOR?"

Miss Fisk broke down, and wept.

"Dear, dear," said the Doctor. " 'Tears, idle tears,' just so. They can hardly have been friends, Inspector, in barely a fortnight. By the by, I ought perhaps to explain that I call all my housekeepers Mrs. Sollihull because I am no good at names, and otherwise it is very confusing. Indeed, they have very queer names, as often as not. This one now, what was her real name . . . ?"

"Could it have been Cuttle?" asked the Inspector, leaning forward in his eagerness. "Because if so, Doctor, believe me, she is much better where she is—dead."

"The postcard certainly was not in the name of Cuttle. Cox, perhaps, or was it Frisby? But why would anyone called Cuttle be better dead?"

"Not better for themselves, Doctor. But better for you. These are deep waters, sir."

"Well, they seem to be. And now, if you could get this lady along to her own premises, perhaps I could resume my work. Oh, wait though—I haven't been to bed yet. Manciple had an hour, earlier on; he sleeps remarkably well, Manciple. I suppose you policemen sleep as and when you can."

"We have our terms of duty, sir. And now, I can do nothing more here at present. It will be all in order for you to go to bed, but please be available later in the day for further questioning. I'll leave a constable here, and I shall have to lock the housekeeper's room. The body has now been removed, of course. Miss

Fisk will come with me, and I will see her safely home. I'd like to have a look at the way along the roof tops. So for the moment, good-bye, sir. Come, Miss Fisk. Wix!"

"What a nice fellow," the Doctor said, after they had all gone, except the constable. "They were all very nice. Now, let me see, I must be methodical. Indeed, I had better write things down. It is Wednesday at nine o'clock. I had better take my bath. Then I will go round to Cakebread's; they must supply another at once."

He undressed and got into bed.

5

One might have overlooked Cakebread's at first, for the entrance was sandwiched between a cutthroat grocer's and a store specializing in surplus army goods and railway lost property; the one was flanked by a pile of tinned milk six feet high marked, "Look! Three tins for two and a penny!" And the other by a number of green-and-yellow gas capes marked, "Ideal for gardening, six hundred only, eighteen and eleven." Somewhere behind all this on the faded door was the brass plate: "By Appointment to H.R.H. Princess Sophey of Gand. Cakebread's. Walk up."

This Dr. Blow did with a purposeful air, ignoring the gas capes and the tinned milk so completely that he all but tipped the latter over with the swing of his overcoat. A few steps behind came Professor Manciple, once more pressed into service as a witness.

Two flights of narrow stairs brought the old gentlemen to a door marked "Cakebread's. Please enter."

"This is it," Blow said, a little breathlessly. "You haven't been here before. They know me very well; I always get them here. Housekeepers—but they have everything, you know: cooks and coachmen and gardeners and butlers and odd jobs. Don't let them get talking about Princess Sophey, though, not if you can help it. Well! I always walk in—ha ha—but I never catch them playing crown and anchor; Tom Warton loved it."

They found themselves at once in the presence of the principal, for Miss Cakebread was dictating a letter to Miss Emily Cakebread, her junior partner and the only surviving member of the original staff of eight. Business in the supply and exchange of superior domestics had declined so sharply that as Mr. Gurney, Mr. Presence, and Miss Workman severally died, Miss Emily Cakebread had found it possible to combine their work with her own at no extra inconvenience; and poor dear Mr. Joseph who had been called up in 1915 had not yet come back.

". . . and, of course, we are most gratified and delighted, dear Lady Orelebar, to learn that you have been so entirely and so completely satisfied with the services of Ethel Harris," Miss Cakebread was saying distinctly, as Dr. Blow came in. ". . . and we are, as always, dear Lady Orelebar—oh, it is Dr. Blow, Emily. We will finish our correspondence later. Good morning, dear Dr. Blow. Domestics attend only by appointment."

"I am not a domestic," Professor Manciple said mildly, "I am Lady Orelebar's second cousin, as a matter of fact, but I'm here this morning with Dr. Blow. Not but what I dare say there's more money in domestic service than in my line of country, eh, Blow?"

"With the extras, and stamps on their cards, and all that, yes," the Doctor agreed. "But look here, Miss Cakebread, and you, too, Miss Emily Cakebread, it's not good enough, you know. A bare fortnight since you said Mrs. Sollihull had the highest of recommendations, including a Crowned Head, . . ."

"Not a Crowned Head, Dr. Blow; we have, alas, no Crowned Heads now with whom we are in direct contact. No. Mrs. Sollihull came with the Highest References, if you speak of Mrs. Carter . . ."

"That was certainly the name. Carter. Yes, it is the same person as on the postcard of Hyde Park Corner that came in the past for her. Naturally, Manciple, I did not read it beyond ascertaining that it was not addressed to me, and it wasn't; it was addressed, as I have said, to Mrs. Carter that was; Mrs. Sollihull, that is; or, rather, was. And that's what I've come about, Miss Cakebread. She's dead, you know. I shall need another."

"I cannot imagine why Mrs. Carter should be dead," Miss Cakebread said severely. "She was in excellent health when she left here. We always insist on that, you know. Mrs. Carter even had all her own teeth, which is very uncommon among the working classes. She has not yet remitted one week's wages as settlement of our little account, ahem. It is unsatisfactory."

"Do you suppose *I* am satisfied? A month's money paid in advance because she said she needed fitting out and now this after a bare fortnight. A new start to be made, even if you can fix me up; and all her things still there, and everything."

"We cannot be responsible after they leave here," Miss Cakebread said.

"Well, I want another," said Dr. Blow.

Miss Cakebread lifted down a large ledger and began turning the pages, discreetly interposing her lean back between the book and her clients. She had known people to look over her shoulder and mentally make a note of the lodgings of domestics and positively lure them after office hours. Dr. Blow, it was true, was an old and constant customer; but that dreadful Lady Orelebar's cousin looked a sharp one, and one never knew.

Miss Emily Cakebread was thinking about the Beyond, and what Mrs. Carter had probably found there. How strange that in the After Life there were no domestics and all souls were the same!

"Well, there's Miss Angell," Miss Cakebread said at last, dubiously.

"Mine is a bachelor establishment," Dr. Blow pointed out.

Miss Emily's pale cheek took a little color, but Miss Cakebread said sharply, "It is a courtesy title. Miss Angell is most respectable and has buried two husbands. But it is confusing to be called Mrs. Tidy and Mrs. Midgley, and awakens old memories. She is very clean, very quiet, and ideally suited, except that she is a little delicate."

"Oh, Christina, you know she has fits," Miss Emily put in. "Naturally, with so good a client as Dr. Blow . . ."

"Emily! Miss Angell does *not* have fits. One isolated fit might happen to anybody. There could be nobody more willing than Miss Angell."

"Look here," the Professor interposed, "anybody can be willing. Is she up to the work, that's the thing? She needs to cook, clean up, do the shopping, see to his socks and that, and generally manage. That's what's wanted."

"Yes, that's what's wanted," Blow echoed, taking courage.

"Every domestic is offered accompanied by Our Guarantee; Dr. Blow knows that."

"Yes, and look at Mrs. Sollihull."

"Mrs. Carter was unfortunate, but her eccentric behavior developed after she passed through our hands."

"Well, send Miss Angell along and I will speak to her. That is reasonable, eh, Manciple? Speak to her; no harm in that. I must say I enjoy the prospect of having an Angel in the House—ha! Patmore, you know."

"An angel was worth about seven shillings," the Professor remarked, following his own line of thought. "That would be something like three pounds twelve and sixpence today."

"It is not much, but I suppose it will do," Miss Cakebread answered, "but he'll have to pay her stamps. And every Thursday afternoon and alternate Sundays. And she has a pet parrot."

Before the Doctor could think of any reply to this intelligence heavy footsteps sounded on the stairs, and with a perfunctory tap at the door Inspector Urry entered.

"Ah, Inspector! I have just engaged a new housekeeper."

"And I, sir, am still interesting myself in the old one. Will you excuse me?"

"Certainly. We had completed our business with Miss Cakebread; but, if I may, I would very much like to remain and learn how you conduct such an inquiry. I have sometimes read of such matters in books—Masterman, you know, Manciple."

"It is irregular, sir, but nothing here will be confidential, I think. I will not stand in the way of your entertainment. Now, Miss Cakebread? I am Inspector Urry of the local police, and I am investigating the death of a woman described as Mrs. Sollihull or Mrs. Carter, who was lately in domestic service with Dr. Blow. I learn from Dr. Blow that this housekeeper was engaged through your agency some two weeks ago. Can you please tell me more about her?"

"Our business is confidential, Officer. It is not usual to discuss past transactions, but I suppose if the woman is dead there can be no positive objection; the account is closed."

"Thank you. Then will you tell me all you know about her? When did she come to you seeking employment? What was then her address?"

"Well . . . we got her through our London associate office, Cooks and Butlers, Limited. It is a system of exchange, you know. If they cannot place people, or if people wish to be placed in our area, they come to us; and we go to them if we have domestics wishing to be placed in London. There is a great network, you know; we have placed people as far away as Torquay, sometimes, through Devon Domestics, you know."

"And what is the address of Cooks and Butlers, Limited?"

"I will ask my secretary to look it up. Emily, will you give the address of Cooks and Butlers to the Inspector?"

"Three hundred Greek Street," said Miss Emily, promptly. "Telephone, Gerrard 38982. Ask for Alf."

"Alf, Emily?"

"I'm sorry, Christina, but I have never learned his full name. He is certainly neither cook nor butler; and, indeed, I have sometimes wondered if those families are now represented in the concern."

"Alf will do nicely," the Inspector said soothingly. "It is unlikely that there is an Alf Cook and an Alf Butler, in any case."

"Alph, the sacred river," Dr. Blow muttered, "very beautiful, very strange. Yes."

"Now, Miss Cakebread, what did you personally see of Mrs. Carter? She attended here for interview and so on?"

"Well, no. Dr. Blow was in urgent need, and Cooks and Butlers sent her straight down to him. I never actually saw her myself."

"But you said she had all her teeth," Manciple protested.

"They were on her card index."

"I suppose the highest recommendations were on that, too?"

"The integrity of our London associates is beyond reproach," Miss Cakebread said icily.

"All the same," Inspector Urry said, "we have no guarantee that the Mrs. Carter whom Dr. Blow engaged was, in fact, the person you recommended and whom your London associates sent down; or, in fact, that they did send anyone down at all."

"We have discharged their account; although, in point of fact, we have received nothing ourselves as yet. Mrs. Carter has not yet paid the week's wages to which we, as negotiating agency, are entitled, and Dr. Blow . . ."

"No satisfaction, no fee. It says so on your letterhead," Blow asserted stoutly. "Mrs. Sollihull was most unsatisfactory. And, anyway, it's only a fortnight; your account is monthly."

"Just so," Miss Cakebread agreed. "I was about to say as much; and, further, that an adjustment would be made."

"You have not yet answered my last question fully," Inspector Urry pointed out. "Did you ever see Mrs. Carter? Can you be sure she was the person who actually turned up at Dr. Blow's house to take the job as housekeeper?

"If she had all her teeth, . . ." Miss Emily began.

"Be quiet, Emily. The Inspector is a busy man. No, if you put it like that, I can't be positive; but Emily is so far right; it is very unusual for them to have all their teeth."

"She had her mouth open when we found her," Dr. Blow pointed out. "They seemed to be there."

"Strong and white, her card says," Miss Emily observed.

"It all helps," the Inspector admitted, as Sergeant Wix noted the fact down. "Indeed, I think we'll borrow the card."

"If it is essential, but otherwise I'd prefer not," Miss Cakebread answered. "You see, it's got somebody else on the back: Mrs. Waters; and we may want to refer to it at any time until we've fixed her up."

"Christina!" Miss Emily put in, excitedly, "would not Mrs. Waters do for Dr. Blow?"

"Dr. Blow has stairs," said Miss Cakebread. Seeing the Inspector's puzzled look, she explained further. "Mrs. Waters is very willing, but she can't have stairs because of her legs."

"I'd rather take the parrot," Blow said.

Inspector Urry put on his hat. "Well!" he said, "thank you, Miss Cakebread. If we really need that index card we'll ask for it. And you'll be hearing from us again, because we shall ask you to sign a statement. But otherwise, I think we shall give you no further trouble."

"We take no responsibility," Miss Cakebread replied.

The four men paused on the pavement outside, and then Inspector Urry said a little grudgingly, "Can I give you gentlemen a lift?"

"We *are* going home," Dr. Blow admitted.

The black police car turned and threaded its way through the busy town center, and so to the comparative quiet of Priory Place. A handful of sightseers stood looking up at the windows of Blow's flat, which had all its blinds decorously drawn. Everybody craned his neck to see the two old gentlemen get out of the police car. "That's him," they told one another.

Blow's fame as an editor of the English poets had never before brought him this sort of recognition, and he enjoyed it. All the same, he was a stickler for correct usage.

"That's *he*," he said to the nearest spectator. *"He!* That's *he,* you know."

The spectator transferred his attention to Professor Manciple, and the rest of the crowd did the same.

"That's him," one of them said to a newcomer.

6

The Chief Constable listened carefully and without interrupting as Inspector Urry made his report. Then he summed it all up: "It amounts to this, then; she'd been dead about eight hours, stabbed by a knife which is missing. We know all about the London end; nothing there, of course. It's virtually certain neither this Dr. Blow nor his professor friend are involved, nor even the lady that borrows nutmeg. It's an outside job. You'll have to trace everybody that goes in and out of the block—ten flats, are there—and especially anybody who went in on the day of the murder. Find out whom the woman knew in the town. Chase about, eh, Urry?"

"That's about it, sir."

"What's this nonsense in the report about Constable Elkins?"

"Nosebleed, sir. He always gets it when he's excited."

"The woman Fisk said he was dead when she examined him."

"She *said* she came to borrow ground almonds," the Inspector pointed out.

"Yes, . . . well, if you're sure Elkins is alive—we'd better concentrate on this Mrs. Sollihull. She's dead enough, anyway. Anything else we can use on her?"

"One thing, sir. Tucked in the top of her stocking was a bit of paper. Here."

The Chief Constable took it, a torn fragment of cheap writing paper with three words on it in capital letters: "FROM THE GREEK."

"Who's the Greek?" he asked.

"I don't know," admitted Inspector Urry. "But I mean to find out. As a matter of fact, that's my next job. A little trip down to the harbor."

"Better take Elkins with you, then. There's nothing like a cold quay for nosebleed."

"Oh, very good, sir! My wife will enjoy that. 'It was nosebleed,' I said, so the Chief Constable said . . .'"

"All right, cut along, Urry."

The Chief Constable began to think how he would recount the joke to *his* wife.

Meanwhile, the two old gentlemen of Priory Place were in Blow's flat drinking tea and waiting for the arrival of Miss Angell.

"I always interview them in the evening," the Doctor was explaining, "because the flat looks smaller in the dark. They think it looks cosy and easy to keep clean. By daylight you can see the hall is nearly thirty feet long and all scrubbed boards. If I've promised once, I've promised a dozen times to get it covered with lino, but they never stay long enough. Is that she?"

"It's impossible to say, Blow, unless you answer the door; it's someone, that's certain."

"Of course, if I don't answer it, it won't be answered! I forget, you know. That's why I need a housekeeper. Come along, we'll soon see—ah! Inspector Urry. Don't tell me you have come to apply for the job?"

"No, sir. I have only one question to ask you. May I come in? Good evening, Professor Manciple. See, gentlemen, I have here a scrap of paper; there can be no harm in your taking it, for it has been tested for fingerprints. Can either of you remember seeing it before?"

"Where did you find it, Inspector?"

"On the body of Mrs. Sollihull."

"From the Greek . . . !"

"Just so."

"What was from the Greek, Inspector?"

"A knife thrust, I should imagine."

"It is hardly an educated hand, Manciple. Certainly it is unknown to me, Inspector. But I must confess the paper appears similar to that which I used for making notes. See, like this."

The Inspector took up a sheet of the cheap quarto paper and compared it with the scrap Blow handed back to him. They appeared identical. "I'll take your specimen, if I may," he said, folding it into his notebook. "If the message was actually written in the flat, it was a bold man who wrote it; especially with his victim lying dead at his feet and you, sir, in the next room."

"Why do you suppose I was in the next room, Inspector?"

"Your housekeeper was murdered between eight and ten o'clock. You have told me you were working at your book all the afternoon and evening and on into the night, until you were roused by feeling hungry at about three o'clock; so you must have been in your room, or at least in the flat."

"How very dreadful. I might have been attacked as well, and I fear I am a mere tyro at self-defense."

"Pooh," said Professor Manciple, "you have to poke your finger in their eye. I've seen it at the pictures."

"And pray what are they doing with *their* fingers all this time?" Blow inquired. "Or don't they go into that at the pictures?"

"You can mock," Manciple answered, "but the fact remains that it is possible to learn, even if you do go to the pictures. I wouldn't be narrow like that in my outlook, even if I didn't happen to find the pictures a very pleasant occasional distraction. There's the bell again."

"I'll go out at the same time," the Inspector said. "Let me know if you remember anything about the Greek, won't you? Good night."

It took Dr. Blow twenty minutes to engage Miss Angell, and it took Miss Angell about two to decide that this was a superior billet, if you didn't mind a lot of nutty conversation. She agreed to start the next week, and to "look in" each day in the meantime.

When she had gone, Professor Manciple said, "You know, William, a man with a wife is saved all this . . ."

"Not if she gets stabbed," Blow objected.

"Well, that can happen to anybody, though admittedly it seldom does. But I mean, look at you—about thirty housekeepers in forty years, and even now you've no guarantee beyond this woman's bare word that she can cook and sew. I've been lucky,

I suppose, with Mrs. Turner since 1922, but I sometimes think the woman has no ambition."

"The only ambitious housekeeper I ever encountered, thank God, was Mrs. Hoptroft; and I don't want to meet any more like her."

"I always somehow envied you that experience, my dear Blow. Life undoubtedly holds mysteries to which we are strangers. There is, indeed, nearer at hand, this mystery of Mrs. Sollihull. Someone did her to death, my dear fellow; and I should resent it, were I situated as you are. It was a liberty to do it in your flat."

"By George, so it was! That way of looking at it hadn't occurred to me; but, of course, you are absolutely right. Trespassing, to call it by no worse name; and if the fellow has taken my copy of the first edition I'd be set far back in my work just at a critical time. I'm more than inclined to look into the business on my own account; these policemen, after all, are limited in their approach. Take that bit of paper, now. Inspector Urry goes off perfectly happily to look for some fellow nicknamed 'The Greek,' as though the man would have left his visiting card tucked in the woman's stocking. But does it not immediately strike you that 'From the Greek' refers to some translation, or at least transliteration, possibly from Hesiod if not from Homer?"

"I confess the thought crossed my mind; but, Blow, who said it was tucked in her stocking? Not the Inspector! Take care, old fellow; with me anything you say is secret, but I've heard of men being hanged for a silly slip of the tongue."

"Well, it wasn't in her hand," the Doctor said, reasonably. "She had no pockets in her dress. And they found the paper. Women carry things in the most unexpected places, but she would hardly have tucked it behind her ear. Really, where it was is inessential; *what* it was is the thing."

"Just so, 'From the Greek' but no more. Scarcely a fragment, Blow; less than the least half-line of Sappho. There will be no glory in editing a new edition, I fear."

"I know at once when you are jesting, Manciple; you always go a little more pink than usual. Ha ha! Very good, almost as good as parts of Erasmus. But answer my question, pray; do you take the thing to be the beginning, or possibly the end, of some version of an epigram in the Anthology, say? Or an attempt to improve on Weir Smith's *Prometheus?*"

"Surely 'From the Greek' is more likely to be part of some such sentence as 'From the Greek Street Agency'? We know the woman had been sent from those people in London. It may have been part of her credentials."

"Then there is only one thing we can do," the Doctor answered; and he brought his fist down with an emphatic bang on the table, so that a spot of ink leaped from the inkwell onto his latest conjectural emendation of the fourteen hundred and sixteenth line of the first canto of part three, "We must go to London."

He got to his feet as he spoke, but Manciple pushed him down again. "In the morning," he said placidly. "It's already after nine o'clock. You don't suppose they work all night, do you?"

"Why not?" said Doctor Blow. "I always do. Can't think in the daytime."

"No—I say, William, I suppose the flat isn't *haunted.* I don't believe in ghosts, of course, but some people do; and there's certainly a very odd noise coming from Mrs. Sollihull's old room. Do you hear it?"

"It can't be the pipes," Blow said, "because they only go when the plug's pulled, and neither you nor I—and there's no wind tonight. Did I ever tell you the time when Bix of Brasenose came and threw pebbles at my windows and I thought it was the Last Judgment? Of course, I was asleep and doubtless not in full command of my faculties. No."

"Perhaps you would know better how to assess the noise in Mrs. Sollihull's room if you were to listen to it," Manciple observed. With this he led the way on tiptoe into the hall and the two of them crouched down at the keyhole of Mrs. Sollihull's door.

There was a choice of several faint sounds to engage their attention. The most persistent was the swishing of linen being dragged from the bed and presumably folded; this is not normally a noticeable sound, but late at night, in a room known to be locked and empty, it commands respect. To it was added the sound of wheezy breathing and a curious shuffling, which turned out to be the friction of soft-soled slippers on the carpet. For a moment there was confusion in the outer passage, because Dr. Blow attempted to apply his ear to the keyhole at the same time that Professor Manciple was approaching it with his eye; and by the time they had sorted themselves out, the sounds within had ceased.

Manciple tried the door. It was locked, just as the police had left it. "Tut!" he said, but Dr. Blow with an air of efficient triumph put up his hand and took a spare key from the ledge above the door frame.

"Always keep one over every door," he explained, "in case of an escape of gas, you know." He unlocked the door and they bundled into the room.

The bed had been stripped completely, the blankets and sheets being piled in the armchair. The gas fire was alight, and sitting in the other armchair, leaning forward to toast a slice of bread, was Miss Fisk. She gave a little giggle and pulled Mrs. Sollihull's eiderdown closer around her shoulders. "I made sure you were out," she explained, "otherwise I'd have knocked."

Professor Manciple advanced a little closer to the fire and said temperately, "I expect you would wish to tell Dr. Blow why you are making toast in his flat."

"Yes, certainly," said the Doctor, "and, incidentally, I'm sure Mrs. Sollihull always turns it over before it gets black like that." And he murmured under his breath, " 'Who would not rather suffer whipping, than swallow toasts of bits of ribbin?' "

"Tche!" exclaimed the lady, snatching the bread and carefully blowing out a little flickering blue flame from one corner before throwing the slice out of the window. "That's the third! I get thinking, you know, and besides this fire is hotter than mine. . . ."

"But yours *is* your own," Manciple prompted gently, "and this one is Dr. Blow's."

"Well, you see, I didn't have a penny for the gas, nor a six-pence, nor even a shilling; my meter has the three slots, you know, not so convenient as you'd think, because in the dark you can easily put the sixpence in the penny slot and then you get nothing. Well, my gas went out and I knew Mrs. Sollihull's room wasn't in use exactly, so I just popped in. I brought my own bread, of course."

"But, my dear lady, the door was locked, and the front door of the flat was locked, too. And the windows are locked, and I am quite certain you didn't come down the chimney."

"The windows are open," Blow observed. "She just threw a piece of toast out of one."

"Of course they are open," Miss Fisk said sharply. "Naturally, I came in that way. No need to rouse Dr. Blow for a little neighborly kindness like the loan of a penn'orth of gas. I slid back the catch with a carving knife and came in."

"I suppose you know that window ledge is about four inches wide and sixty feet about the ground?"

"I wasn't there long enough to get cold and I'm wearing an extra wooly."

Dr. Blow suddenly decided to take a hand; after all, it was his flat and Manciple was too fond of doing all the talking. "Miss Fisk," he said firmly, "I must tell you that I find your action distinctly eccentric. I am not a hasty man, but I must ask you —I think I may ask you this without implied impropriety— what were you doing to the bed clothes of the late Mrs. Sollihull's bed?"

"I thought she might have left her watch under her pillow."

"But you were not boiling an egg."

"I don't need a watch for that. I hum three verses of 'For all the Saints.' But I wanted to be back for 'Today in Parliament' at ten forty-five."

Both gentlemen consulted their watches.

"You've just time," said the Professor, "but I hardly like to see you climb up the wall carrying a plate of toast."

"Unless she slings it round her neck," interposed Dr. Blow. "I'm almost certain I know of a piece of strong twine. But I am quite willing for her to go out by the front door."

Miss Fisk turned out the gas. "I'm always most careful," she said. "There is nothing quite so dangerous as an escape of gas."

The Doctor nodded his agreement.

When she had gone, Dr. Blow looked at his watch. "Just as I thought," he said, "my watch has stopped. I didn't like to say anything, but I felt you were hurrying her off rather abruptly, Manciple, if her wireless talk was at ten forty-five, though I suppose the machinery has to be wound up. It's only nine now by my watch; but, of course, if it has stopped, it may well be much later. I wonder if Mrs. Sollihull *did* leave her watch under her pillow? There might be no real harm in my borrowing it until my own is wound up."

"It isn't under her pillow now," Manciple remarked, "and I don't suppose it was under her pillow then. I distrust that woman, Blow. When you look under a pillow you don't need to rip a long hole in the mattress with a carving knife."

"I had a feeling all along that those were feathers," said the Doctor. He sneezed violently.

7

"Where is the engine?" asked Dr. Blow. "I know we are not traveling to Bath, Manciple, but I always ask. One of the stations at Bath is a cul-de-sac and they steam in and back out; so that if you came from Cheltenham facing the engine, you arrive ultimately at Bournemouth with your back to it. And vice versa, if you are going the other way, unless at Bath you change over; and often there is someone sitting there."

"They might care to change, too, Blow."

"I sometimes ask, if I am feeling skittish, but travelers today are much less obliging than formerly. I remember once on a bitterly cold night at Mangotsfield when I had to change and the waiting room was on fire. . . ."

"I can't see any engine," said Manciple. "It must be an electric train. And if we don't get in at once we shan't see any train, either. That man is waving a flag."

"But we came purposely twenty minutes early. . . ."

"Get in, man, get in!"

When they were seated in the train and the streets and roofs of the town were giving place to open fields Blow suddenly said excitedly, "I am sure we leave that large church spire on our right when we go to London! It's gone past on the left. You had better pull the communication cord, Manciple."

"I haven't five pounds to spare, thank you."

"Or do you leave it on the left *coming back* from London?"

"Blow, you mustn't be a fidget; we have other things to think about. I suggest that you leave it on your right when you are sitting with your back to the engine, or to the front if it be an electric train; and on your left when you are sitting opposite. We can't be *coming from* London, surely you know that. And we are leaving the town behind."

"Just so," said Dr. Blow. "It is most confusing. I hope you have the tickets, Manciple. And did you pay the extra for the insurance. I read somewhere that in the Chaldon disaster only two were covered by the insurance and one had the ticket tucked in his hat."

"You'd better tuck yours in your hat, then."

"Really, Manciple, I am surprised sometimes at the poor taste of your jests. I am in no sense nervous, I assure you."

For a few miles they sat in silence, Manciple smoking his pipe and Blow occasionally taking a peppermint. Then the Professor knocked the ash out of his pipe and uncrossed one knee from above the other and spoke.

"I've been thinking about that Miss Fisk, Blow," he observed. "How does a woman like that live? You can't exist on what you can borrow next door. But nobody these days has an income worth anything, unless they work. I think it is very strange indeed."

"I wouldn't give her another thought," said Dr. Blow. "Don't think me gross, but what real idea can one have of the lady when she gets herself up like that. She may well be uncommonly skinny. You're better off as you are."

"Don't be a fool, Blow. I'm only trying to establish *a motive*. Mrs. Sollihull was killed, if you remember; and every so often this Miss Fisk mysteriously appears in your flat with some thin explanation of her presence. Making toast, indeed. I suppose you noticed she hadn't brought any butter? But everyone knows toast is no good buttered cold."

"Perhaps she was relying on using mine."

"And that carving knife. You don't need a carving knife to force back the catch of a window. A penknife will do. I've got into Magdalen scores of times. . . . *But you do need a carving knife to stab someone in the back*."

"You can use that thing for taking stones out of horses' hooves."

"And another thing, Blow. When she ripped open that mattress. She wasn't looking for any watch. She had a watch on her wrist under her sleeve. I saw it."

"Did you see if it was Mrs. Sollihull's?"

"No, I didn't. But I tell you this; the key to this mystery is in your flat, and probably in that mattress!"

"Then why are we going up to London, Manciple?"

"Because London will probably furnish the lock. A key in a mattress does nobody any good. It needs to be in a lock."

"Not if it's a watch key," said Dr. Blow. "You must excuse my little joke, Manciple. A railway journey always makes me frivolous. But I am sure you are right, very right. The woman is not everything she seems or purports to be. It was unfriendly to interfere with the mattress even though not in use. Miss Angell will need it; I only hope she's handy with a needle. Putting the feathers back will be a bit of a job, too. I remember when we tarred and feathered the Founder's statue—I forget just why, offhand—I kept finding feathers in my hair weeks after, and I was most scrupulous about shampoos."

"If everything goes as I expect, that mattress will be needed as evidence. Miss Angell must have another, Blow. She may have to have another gas fire, too. The police are very insistent, I know. They produce everything in court. Ah—this will be London, I think."

"Greek Street?" said the policeman. "Take a thirteen to Piccadilly Circus and walk up Shaftesbury Avenue, or a number seven to Oxford Street and get off at Soho Square and walk down."

"Second left," said the policeman in Shaftesbury Avenue, "and mind how you cross, sir. This isn't Tithing-cum-Boring."

"Extraordinary," said Blow. "We should have taken that constable's number. He was quoting Macaulay, Manciple."

"If you had taken better heed to his matter than to its derivation you wouldn't have been nearly run over by that taxi, Blow. He had every right to call you what he did, that driver."

"Well, well, our jaunt mustn't be marred by a little foul language, Manciple! And here, surely, is Greek Street. There seem to be a great many young men unemployed in these parts. Let us ask one of them if he can direct us to the Greek Street Agency and earn sixpence. Er, . . . I wonder if you could advise me?"

At the junction of Greek Street and Old Compton Street there were about twenty young, and youngish, men standing idly around talking. All had their hands in their trousers pockets and cigarettes depending from their lips, and they talked without moving their mouths very much, using laconic monosyllables and a good deal of puzzling jargon. Dr. Blow wondered if some of them might be foreign, especially when the first one shrugged his shoulders wearily and turned away.

"Try French," suggested Manciple.

Blow tried French; after this he tried Italian, and a little audience began to form.

"Proper gent, ain't he?" one young man asked another.

"They are making game of you, Blow," the Professor observed. "Come along. It ought not to be beyond our powers to find number three hundred. We are already opposite number sixteen, you will notice."

"Do you know, Manciple, I believe those were what they call Teddy Boys," Blow remarked, as they went along.

"Two hundred and sixty-two," answered Manciple, counting, "two-six-three—we are making steady progress. Surely it must be that one two doors from the one painted yellow."

The house two doors from the one painted yellow was almost entirely innocent of paint of any color. It was one of the older houses in the street, and had apparently not been touched, except by time, since it left the hands of the builder around 1680. The plain brick façade was nearly black and the windows were grimy. The crumbling woodwork still bore some traces of carving round the doorway, and a delicate shell-shaped fanlight above contained three panes of glass and four of brown paper. Just inside the narrow passageway behind the front door was a faded notice board with several names: "Gunstein and Gunstein, Theatrical Agents"; "S. H. Welsh, Commission Agent"; "Mr. Cartland"; and "The Greek Street Agency: Cooks and Butlers, Ltd."

"Fourth floor, that's the top," Manciple said. "How these domestic servants cling to their attics! We had better begin to climb."

On the second landing Blow clutched his friend's arm. "Manciple, my dear fellow," he whispered, "did you chance to come armed?"

"Armed?"

"Oh well, never mind. I have my Uncle Arthur's police whistle."

"Blow, surely you understand that the days of police whistles are over? The police have something better to do than come running every time someone whistles. Even taxi drivers don't bother any more. And you wouldn't get a taxi with a thing like that. It's an anachronism. Dear me, I am doubtful if they even use them now in the Boy Scouts."

"I feel happier, Manciple, with *something*. Well, let's go in!"

Cooks and Butlers, Ltd. was a very different establishment from its affiliated agency, Cakebread's; and yet it had its points of similarity, too. It was in a suite of two rooms; the front room, into which Manciple now led the way, being the general office, overlooked Greek Street—except that the narrow windows were set somewhat below the ornamental coping that crowned the façade, and there was little to be seen but the blank walls of the back of a film company's offices in the next street. The back room overlooked roofs and more roofs, always a picturesque prospect, except that the prevailing southwest winds had driven so much smoke against the glass that it was almost impossible to see out. In this room, Manciple could see through the open door, sat a sallow young man in his late twenties with his feet on a rolltop desk and a telephone receiver to his ear. A cigarette hung from his lip all the while he was talking. He waved a negligent hand to the visitors and carried on.

Dr. Blow moved to the window and said, "We must not listen, Manciple, for that would be most impolite. But did you hear him say he had twenty ounces pure and another fifty to put through. Surely even the underservants are not supplied by weight? I am jesting, you know."

"I know," said Manciple. "I'm not the only one that goes

pink. But all the same, and even if it is rude, I mean to listen. So pray don't engage me in conversation for a moment, my dear fellow. This may be important."

"Just as you say, but as we shall not have any further large opportunity of speaking, let me tell you of a happy thought that has just struck me. Let us prosecute our inquiries as though we were police officers! Then we shan't have to enact any foolish farce of pretending to want to engage a domestic—eh?"

Professor Manciple's determination to listen was now frustrated by the young man's ringing off.

"Yes?" he said, taking one foot off the desk as a concession to the arrival of prospective clients. "If it's for Alf, he's out."

"We are police officers," Blow said severely. "Not, of course, uniformed men, as you can see; but detectives, you know. From the Yard."

In his time the young man had seen a great many detectives of one sort and another, but he said nothing more than, "Yes?"

"Chief Detective Superintendent . . . er . . . Smith," Dr. Blow amplified. "This is Chief Detective Sergeant Robinson."

"I suppose you have a search warrant?" suggested the young man.

"Oh, naturally. I have it in a small frame in my bedroom. Robinson has one, too; I've seen it. And now for our questions."

"Allow me, sir," said Manciple. He pulled out a pencil and an old envelope, on the face of which was clearly written: Professor Gideon Manciple. "What is your name, young man?"

"Do I have to answer that?"

"It would be polite," Blow interposed. "We have identified ourselves to you."

"Bernard Shaw. Bernie, they call me."

"Well, now, Bernie," said Manciple, writing rapidly, "is there anyone here called 'The Greek'?"

"No, sir."

"Just as I thought, Manciple," said Blow. "The whole theory was absurd. Probably she'd just been amusing herself with my little Anacreon; there's one quite handy in the dining room where anyone could see it. Of course, I am most particular that they must not touch my books in the study, but there could be no harm at all—and it was her afternoon off—in just borrowing the parallel text and trying to improve on the English version here and there."

"Be quiet, Chief Super. The Chief Super is in disguise, you know," Manciple explained, hurrying on with his questions. "Do you know a domestic called Elsie, possibly Elsie Cuttle?"

"I'm almost certain it was Carter on the card," Blow put in.

"What sort of a domestic?" said the young man, to gain time.

"A housekeeper. She was supplied to a Dr. Blow through Cakebread's Agency, who obtained her, it is said, through you."

"She had all her teeth," added Blow, helpfully.

"All our housekeepers have all their teeth," the young man said. "We have our pride."

"Well?" said Manciple.

"Not to know her, like," the young man said. "You see, I'm not on the staff. I'm a page boy in between situations. It's Alf you need, really."

"And where is Alf?"

"Like I said," said the young man, "he's out. Unless this is him."

Heavy footsteps outside heralded the arrival of Alf, breathing hard, who was a stout man in a smart blue suit.

"Jim," he said, hurrying in, "there's a rozzer's car up the street and Dolly says—oh! Who's this?"

"Police," said the young man, with possibly the suggestion of a wink. "Looking for a housekeeper called Elsie Cuttle or Carter, with sound teeth."

"Not looking for her," Blow explained. "We know where she is. Asking about her, that's all. Are you Alf?"

"Who wants to know?"

"We have called at the instance of Miss Emily Cakebread," Manciple said. "And, of course, in pursuance of our official duties . . ."

"Just so," said Dr. Blow.

". . . to make certain inquiries concerning a housekeeper named Cuttle or possibly Carter sent from this agency to a Dr.

Blow, who is a client of Cakebread's Agency."

"And what are the inquiries?"

"Er . . . well, inquiries, you know."

"They already know she had all her teeth," the young man said as helpfully as he could.

"I don't know no Elsie Cuttle, thank you. Nor Carter. And now, if you gentlemen will allow me, I will continue with my day's business. And you can tell Miss Emily Cakebread . . ."

"*Flash* Elsie," said Manciple suddenly, leaning forward.

"Jim," said Alf, "you better lock the door."

Dr. Blow drew out his police whistle.

"Now, gentlemen," said Alf, "suppose you sit down. I don't like your manner. 'Flash Elsie,' you say, full of meaning, and one of you pulls out a police whistle. Let me make you a little speech. First, this is a respectable domestic agency. We don't supply housekeepers with nicknames. Next, you two ain't police officers. We are on the most cordial terms with the authorities, let me tell you. Know 'em all. I was having a drink with the Commissioner only last week at Lord Havergal's. Nice fellow, that. Next, you try to claim acquaintance with one of our most respected associates, Miss Emily Cakebread. As it happens, I have recently left Miss Emily Cakebread, and she told me all about you. Con men, that's what you are."

"Con men? What an extraordinary expression!"

"Or narks."

"Narks?"

"Nix, narks; you ain't got the intelligence. I suppose you're that Dr. Blow. Well, let me tell you, Dr. Blow, you'll get no more housekeepers from me; you don't look after 'em. And I've advised Miss Cakebread, too. We have our reputation, just like them. And our professional pride."

"I told them," the young man said eagerly.

"You also said your name was Bernard Shaw," Professor Manciple reminded him.

"*James* Bernard Shaw," said the young man. "Why not?"

"He was named after his Uncle James," Alf acknowledged.

"That's very reasonable," Dr. Blow observed judicially, "especially if there were expectations. The lower classes often display a keen sense of the family, especially when there are expectations. I can believe that his name is James, Manciple."

"You can get out now," Alf said, without heat but firmly. "And you needn't call again. Jim, unlock the door. Good day, gentlemen. You will excuse me seeing you to the lift; I might be tempted to kick you downstairs."

Jim unlocked the door and threw it open. "After you, Chief Detective Superintendent," he said mockingly. The two old gentlemen moved out onto the landing, feeling a little crestfallen, and the door slammed. They heard the key turn behind them.

"Clump down with as much noise as you can," Manciple whispered, "while I pretend to tie my shoelace." He bent down with his ear to the keyhole, and Dr. Blow began to descend the stairs. Manciple was rewarded with this illuminating snatch of conversation.

"Ring up Sneider, quick."

"D'ye think they suspected?"

". . . just two old fools, but better be on the safe side."

"Elsie. . . ."

The Professor crept away.

When he reached the street Dr. Blow was nowhere to be seen, nor was there any immediate place in which he could have concealed himself, no shop close by; the only nearby turning led into a cul-de-sac; no taxi in sight, and no crowded pavement among whose throngs he might be hidden; an almost empty street, in fact.

As Manciple hesitated on the threshold, his friend tapped him on the shoulder from behind. "Hist!" he whispered, dramatically, "a piece of great good fortune, Manciple. I foolishly missed the street door in the dark, you know. I was wondering if, in fact, she would have bothered with Anacreon, not a woman's poet, you know, and I just went on going down the stairs without thinking. So I found myself in the basement; it's easily done. I had to visit the *Times* newspaper once, and the same thing happened, . . . yes. Well, come and see what I have discovered!"

He urged the Professor before him into the dark passage again and down a creaking flight of stairs into a damp and pitch dark lobby.

"Don't strike a match," he warned. "Somebody may see us. Now, here! I thought it was the street door, but it wasn't."

He pushed Manciple into a black hole and the door swung to behind them. A faint light came into the place through a barred window, which lay apparently almost directly under the street. In the gloom Manciple saw a bench and a certain amount of what appeared to be machinery. On the bench were piled several dozens of knives and forks and other domestic articles. At one side was a heavy duty electric wire attached to a heavy square object rather like a large biscuit tin. "Electric furnace," Blow explained. "I've seen them in the Army & Navy Stores catalogue. *It melts things down. . . .*"

"We'd better get out of here before they melt us down!"

"That was what he meant by twenty ounces pure," the Doctor said, shaking his head. "I suspected that the young man was not being frank with us. I am very much afraid we have stumbled upon an illicit traffic in silver."

"Don't you wish you really were a Chief Detective Superintendent?" asked the Professor. "Then you might get promoted!"

"We must be very practical now," Blow replied, severely. "Creep up the stairs and don't sneeze or anything. We may be in grave danger!"

Whatever the danger, they survived it, and three minutes later were hurrying down Greek Street toward Shaftesbury Avenue. Only the elder Gunstein saw them go, from the window of his theatrical agency. "Professor types," he thought, "but they're overdoing it. I wonder who they really are. Cops, I suppose. Well, we got nothing to fear!"

Three floors above, Alf was dialing a number.

8

"We'd better go to the club," said the Doctor, stepping into the road and waving his hand vigorously to a distant taxi. "But mine was bombed—I remember they wrote to me. I wonder where we are accommodated now?"

"Perhaps the driver knows," Manciple observed, getting into the cab.

"Ah, yes," said Dr. Blow. "We want to go to my club, or possibly to Manciple's, only that's rather far. Suppose you drive along slowly while we decide."

"I know a nice little place in Knightsbridge," said the driver hopefully.

"That would be handy for the V & A," Manciple contributed. "But we can't go anywhere, Blow, unless you get into the cab."

Twenty minutes later they were sitting in a quiet corner of the vast, shadowy smoking room of Professor Manciple's club, with two large glasses of the club port before them.

"We must make a progress report," the Professor had said, taking several sheets of the club letter paper.

Dr. Blow was watching him with keen interest. "I can't help thinking, Manciple," he was saying, "that you show an uncommon aptitude for police work. In some respects it is a pity it was not *your* housekeeper who was stabbed, although she is a nice woman. Then I could have gone forward with my work. As it is, I suppose you need me."

"Certainly I need you. Your support is invaluable. Now, Blow, listen to this. It represents a précis of available information so far. Much curtailed, of course; just the heads, you know."

" 'I only give the heads' . . . , but, in fact, Byron was somewhat prolix. I trust you will be less so."

"You shall judge."

Taking a preliminary mouthful of the wine, Manciple began. "Late evening of Tuesday: Mrs. Sollihull stabbed. Early morning of Wednesday: her body discovered by Dr. Blow. Authority: Dr. Blow and medical evidence."

"Witness: Manciple," the Doctor put in. "I was most careful."

"Clues," Manciple went on, "one knife, instrument of death, subsequently mislaid. One piece of paper marked 'From the Greek.' "

"There ought to be more clues than that," protested Dr. Blow. "The police were in her room long enough."

"Well, there's the medical evidence, and the information gathered since, and whatever the police may know that they have not communicated to us; but, in essentials, all we know about the crime is that she is dead, that the knife has disappeared, and that there is a bit of paper which you said was tucked into her stocking. That was suspicious, Blow, whatever you say."

"If you take that position, Manciple, I shall have to remind you that the words 'From the Greek' were *indubitably in your handwriting*. I only said it was an uneducated hand to protect you from the questioning of the police."

"My dear Blow, if I wrote the words 'From the Greek,' I should write them in Greek. And my Greek is hardly up to sustained translating these days. A little Aeschylus, perhaps, purely as a relaxation now and then. But that is all."

"I felt sure the matter had no connection with that little Anacreon of mine. . . . Well, go on."

"Wednesday and thereafter: police routine investigations proceeding. At least, we may assume so. With these we have, of course, nothing to do. But a parallel investigation privately conducted by Professor Manciple and Dr. Blow, in the disinterested pursuit of pure truth . . ."

". . . and because we like a jaunt . . ."

". . . established the following additional facts: That Miss Fisk is much interested in the contents of Mrs. Sollihull's mattress.

That Mrs. Sollihull's watch may or may not be missing, along with the knife with which she was stabbed. And that the Greek Street Agency for domestics has an illicit furnace in the cellar."

"Hardly illicit, Manciple. Such furnaces are not against the law or I shouldn't have seen them in the Army & Navy Stores catalogue."

"Be that as it may, a domestic servants' agency can have no obvious use for such an instrument. And, incidentally, your Army & Navy Stores catalogue was issued in 1902, if it's the thing I have seen in your flat with no covers and an advertisement for Epp's Cocoa."

"You can't get that now, you know, Manciple. So smooth, so nourishing—and guaranteed instantly soluble."

"Not like this crime of ours, Blow, which appears essentially insoluble, ha, ha! Another glass of port, my dear fellow? And let's say no more about where that scrap of paper was, hey? Or the handwriting."

"We must certainly not be suspicious of one another, unless indeed all else fails. Yes, the port is excellent. I think our next line of inquiry ought to concern your friend Miss Fisk, Manciple; but first, what do you think we ought to do about that electric furnace? If it is not an illegal possession, it is at least an unusual one in a domestic agency, unless they use it for casting sets of teeth. They seem to make an uncommon point about teeth in their upper servants, although I am bound to say they seem to have been less scrupulous in the case of that young page boy."

"I think our present function is to gather information and not to give it. It would be uncommonly amusing to be able to go along to that fellow Urry and say, 'Inspector, we have solved the mystery for you!' How his face would fall! I am not motivated by malice, you know. But people too freely think we academic fellows don't know what's what, you know. And besides, there is a strange excitement in the quest, is there not? Like deciphering the inscription on an unknown groat of the fourteenth century. . . ."

"Butler never refers to them, you know. But, of course, the issue was discontinued after 1662."

"Drink your port, Blow. These are irrelevancies; we must get home. There's no knowing what sort of a field day Miss Fisk is having in your flat."

From the wide eighteenth-century bow windows of the harbormaster's office it was possible to see every ship in the harbor, for this was no Liverpool or Southampton. The harbormaster himself was correspondingly less busy, and he sat with a pint of beer at his elbow and with a pipe of tobacco comfortably between his teeth, with Inspector Urry similarly employed in the easy chair opposite. Sergeant Wix had his notebook open, but he, too, was provided with beer and comforts. The sun shone, and a distant siren told maritime secrets to the initiated.

"That's the *Sandchuck* now," said the harbormaster. "Tide's making. She'll be able to cross the bar in another twenty minutes. Be alongside Appleby's wharf by three."

"We can run over what you've told us while we're waiting. Carry on, Wix."

Sergeant Wix read slowly. "Information supplied by Captain Crashaw, harbormaster, concerning movements of shipping, etc., on the twenty-fifth, -sixth, and -seventh. Ships now in harbor that were in harbor then: three—*Sally Lunn,* laid up, no crew, only a watchman; *Stalbridge,* discharging timber, Fanshawe's wharf; *Mist of Time,* collier, Gas Works wharf. Crew lists appended. But no Greek seaman among them, and no seaman nicknamed 'The Greek.' Ships in harbor on the night of the crime and since sailed: six—*Aster,* collier, for Cardiff (there by now); *Octoroon,* in ballast for Marseilles, she can be contacted by radio; *Trixie* and *French Horn,* colliers, for Barrow, can be reached at Barrow tomorrow or next day at latest; *Coronet,* for Copenhagen, contact by radio; *Viper,* for Falmouth, already there, contact through local authorities; and *Sandchuck,* which left for Erith on the twenty-sixth and has just returned with cement and is now entering harbor."

"Obviously, *Sandchuck* is our first call," said the Inspector. "By the time we get down there, she'll be in, eh, Harbormaster?"

"Just about. Come on then, gentlemen. Let's see, she carries eight hands and three officers, and of course the engine-room people, another ten—crew of twenty-one. Captain Forbes, master. Nobody would ever venture to call *him* Greek, so you need interrogate only twenty."

The three men strolled slowly along the quays toward Appleby's wharf. One man sat there on a coil of rope, smoking. He nodded to the harbormaster and slowly got to his feet, picking up the looped rope from under him.

The ship was coming in at a walking pace, hardly a ripple at her bow. She began to swing, her single screw churning up the dirty harbor water in a brown froth like that on the head of a glass of stout. A man on the forecastle lifted his hand negligently and the man on the wharf suddenly flung his end of rope. For the first time he moved swiftly, and before the cable began to tighten he was at the other end of the ship, flinging another. A donkey engine clanked for a moment, edging the *Sandchuck* in. And then for a moment there was silence, and in the silence they distinctly heard an officer's voice down below: "Where's that bloody Greek?"

The deeply laden ship rode level with the wharf, and Inspector Urry stepped aboard.

". . . and that's all I can tell you," concluded Captain Forbes. "But by all means talk to the men. Use my cabin here, if you like. But I've got to go ashore, if you'll excuse me." He rose to his feet, nodded in a friendly way, and departed.

He had told Inspector Urry nothing he didn't already know. The ship had left harbor on the night of the twenty-fifth/twenty-sixth, just about the time that Dr. Blow was beginning to feel hungry. She had proceeded empty to Erith and had there taken on a cargo of cement, which she brought back today—and here she was. A regular, routine trip. It was true he had a man they called "The Greek," but . . .

"Ah!" the Inspector had chipped in, "no 'buts,' please, Captain. It is my duty to see the man, you know."

"See him, then, and welcome," the Captain had answered.

"See them all, by all means. You know your business best, Inspector."

And so, one by one, the crew was questioned. And Inspector Urry, with a fine sense of the dramatic and an iron self-control, kept the man they called "The Greek" until last. Finally, in he came, a stout, dark-skinned man chewing tobacco.

The Inspector asked him his name and his position—he was a stoker—and one or two routine questions, and then he said, "Where were you on the night of the twenty-sixth?"

"I went to the pictures," said "The Greek."

"Tell me about it. What time did you go; what time did you come out; what film did you see; and at what cinema? I'd like you to tell me all the details of the evening."

"Well, see, I had some fried fish about five; then, when they opened, I had maybe two pints, or say three. Then I went along about seven to the Odeon and in I went to the two and ten-pennies. Saw two big films and the news and a cartoon—the whole program. Came out about twenty to eleven and found the pubs shut. So I went to the Seamen's Home and had a bite and played billards until ha'past eleven. Then I turned in."

"What films?"

"Dormant Desire was one, about this chap, see, who loves a girl and never finds out until she's getting married to this other chap—Bick Rudman played him. Well, so he hits Bick Rudman at the entrance to the church; and, of course, Bick Rudman hits him back; and the girl screams because she suddenly realizes which is the one she loves, see?"

"Yes. Of course, if you had seen the film the day before, you would know the plot. I wonder if you can produce evidence that you were in the cinema that particular night. Ticket stub, for example."

"Are you accusing me of anything?"

"Certainly not. But in the course of our investigations we find it necessary to check the movements of the crew of this ship, and it is much easier for us if you are able to offer proof of the accuracy of your statements. And if you went to the cinema, there can be no harm in producing the ticket stub, if you have it."

"Well, I haven't."

"Well, never mind. Now, do you know anyone called Elsie Carter?"

"I used to know a Mavis Carter. That girl! She . . ."

"Elsie, this one."

"No."

"You persist in this denial?"

"Yes."

"Then we'll change the subject again. The film *Dormant Desire* was not showing at the Odeon on the night of the twenty-sixth. What have you to say to that?"

"It was. I saw it."

"Show him the newspaper, Wix."

Sergeant Wix drew a folded newspaper from his pocket. "'Ere," he said, not unkindly. "List of attractions. All this week—and that goes for the twenty-sixth, see, because this is dated the twenty-fifth—Odeon: *Rock 'n' Roll Blues.*"

The Greek looked at the paper closely and then handed it back.

"What about it?" he asked. "I'm talking about the Odeon, Gravesend."

"What!"

"The Odeon, Gravesend. Day I was discharged from the *Ocean Lady,* out of Lagos with tunny fish and figs. First thing I do always is go to the pictures."

"Then you weren't here on the night of the twenty-sixth as part of the *Sandchuck's* crew?"

"No. Signed on just before she sailed to come back. Lost a man who broke his leg taking in coal. I took his place; didn't the Cap'n tell you?"

"No, but he tried," said Sergeant Wix.

Inspector Urry said slowly, "I suppose the man you replaced wasn't called 'The Greek,' by any chance. Not two of you, eh?"

"No. Nor Carter, nor Cuttle neither."

"I'll tell you one thing, son," said the Inspector. "Stoking is a good solid trade. Don't you ever join the police."

"Ain't such a fool," said "the Greek," meaning no offence. He shifted his quid with the intention of spitting, and thought better of it. Captain Forbes had a Turkey carpet which showed every mark.

As they walked back to the car, where Constable Elkins was patiently waiting and enjoying the sea air, Inspector Urry said meditatively, "You know, Wix, when a senior officer comes a cropper, it's as well not to betray amusement."

"Yes, sir."

"Even better not to tell the other chaps."

"Of course not, sir."

"Shall I tell you why?"

"Sir."

"Because sometimes it isn't such a cropper after all. I expect you noticed the remarkable thing about 'the Greek's' knife sheath? It was poking out from under his jersey."

"Sir?"

"There wasn't a knife in it. And did you notice when he said the injured stoker's name wasn't Carter, he went on to say it wasn't Cuttle either? Never say more than you need when you answer questions. And never, never, Wix, be the first to introduce the name of the person who's dead. 'Nor Cuttle neither,' said 'The Greek,' clever-like. 'I was at the Odeon, Gravesend,' he says, pretty smart. But the Odeon, Gravesend, isn't the only place where you can learn the plot of a film by heart, and the twenty-sixth isn't the only night of the week when you can do it. That film was at our Odeon the week before, did you know that?"

"Yes," said Sergeant Wix. "And I can tell you this; it's lousy."

"Like 'The Greek's' story," said Inspector Urry.

9

Miss Angell had arrived and was "settling down." That is to say, she had sewn up the late Mrs. Sollihull's mattress, and made the bed, and had installed her parrot where he could see everything that passed in the big outside world and say rude things to the sea gulls. And she had punctually served to Dr. Blow a succession of meals, all of which he had consumed without comment, as was his habit. Food to the Doctor was merely fuel, intended to provide the energy required in wrestling with the author of *Hudibras*. Of course, toasted cheese was another matter, but Miss Angell hadn't tried that yet.

Dr. Blow had put the affair of Mrs. Sollihull so completely from his mind that he was actually calling Miss Angell, Miss Angell, when he spoke to her, which wasn't often. The Doctor was not unsociable, but he was busy. Sir Hudibras demanded attention undivided.

In forgetting his late housekeeper Dr. Blow had been assisted by the absence of Professor Manciple, who had been obliged by a long-standing engagement to go to Paris and deliver an address at the Sorbonne about the interrelated currencies of France and England in the time of Edward III, a matter which was the occasion of absorbed interest in the minds of twelve people and of polite attention in the other two hundred and nine of his audience.

But even such academic junketings have their surcease, and one fine morning about noon the Professor came tapping at Dr. Blow's door.

"Blow," he said, almost before he was in the room, "a most

extraordinary thing. I went to have my hair cut and while I was waiting I picked up a very old newspaper. The man apologized and said he had all the latest papers and this one had really been brought in to light the fire. He seemed very upset because they had lighted the fire with some paper he hadn't yet read, but I told him that the very little in a daily newspaper that is of permanent interest remains so, very naturally. And as the old copy I held had not previously come to my notice I was perfectly happy to be reading it while I waited."

"Yes, yes, perfectly reasonable, Manciple. But a somewhat trivial anecdote, my dear fellow. Hardly worth bringing to me surely?"

"Blow, you seldom give me an opportunity of concluding any remarks I initiate. You are both impulsive and intolerant of other speakers. This was but the preamble, Blow. More is to follow. In the old newspaper I found this." The Professor then drew out his wallet, and after a little searching produced a very small news clipping, which he handed to Dr. Blow. The Doctor opened a drawer and rummaged for a moment, and at last laid hold of a large reading glass. He began deliberately to read.

". . . if Wolves can make seven points from four matches, they are safe; but Spurs need only six from three matches. Wolves, however, have won four consecutive games and are on the top of their form, whereas Spurs in their last five matches have lost three and won only one—I say, Manciple, this is a little puzzling. . . ."

"You're reading the back of it, Blow! It is the piece on the other side headed 'Odd Occurrence at Arundel' to which I invite your attention."

"I beg your pardon. I thought this appeared to refer to football or ice hockey or some such preoccupation; but it is your own fault, Manciple, if I tried to square it with your known principles. For you are so notorious a supporter of the picture palace, you know, that I fancied this mania for keeping up with the times must have extended itself in you. Just so. Let me see, yes, 'Odd Occurrence at Arundel.' I had an old aunt at Arundel once, and in my irreverent youth I tried hard to introduce her into a limerick, but there are hardly any rhymes, you know. Scarcely any.

Ah, . . . 'Police at Arundel, in Sussex, are investigating a curious incident at the house of Major Atkinson, the well-known writer on military history.'—that must be Atkinson of Queen's—'On Saturday night his housekeeper's room was entered while dinner was being served and the mattress ripped from top to bottom. Nothing else was interfered with. There was a similar incident at Fowey a fortnight ago.' Why were they serving dinner in the housekeeper's bedroom, Manciple? It is indeed curious."

"Blow, they were not serving dinner there. The newspaper writer is trying to make it clear that the housekeeper was absent from her room and the household engaged in other affairs at the time of the incident. It is the ripping of the mattress that is curious. *What happened to Mrs. Sollihull's mattress, eh?*"

"That is hardly the same thing, Manciple. We know that Miss Fisk was looking for Mrs. Sollihull's watch. And Miss Angell has since sewn it up with great neatness. It never got into the newspapers, and this clipping distinctly refers to a house at Arundel."

"I have another clipping here. I had to go to Colindale to consult files of the Cornish newspapers, and then I had to write to Truro and send sixpence for a back number. But I did it, and here is the result."

Professor Manciple produced a second newspaper article. *"Fowey Independent,"* he explained, "founded in 1806. Not the sort of journal to be stampeded into sensationalism."

Dr. Blow took the piece and gave a short laugh. "I can see at once the paragraph to which my attention is invited," he said, "for the recto of this clipping carries part of an advertisement for ploughshares and muck spreaders. With these we have nothing to do, we men of letters. Of course, it is admirable to make two blades of grass grow. . . ."

"Get on with it, William."

"Of course, your time is of value, I know. Pray excuse me if I need sometimes to be recalled to immediacy. Just so, it is here: 'On Friday evening, while Dr. and Mrs. Wheeler were at a bridge party and their domestic staff were watching television, intruders broke into "The Elms" and ripped the mattress on the house-keeper's bed from top to bottom. Nothing was taken, and the police suspect hooligans. Inquiries are going forward.' "

"I dare say. Now, Blow, those two incidents occurred about eighteen months ago. Since then I have ascertained that three other housekeepers have had their beds attacked: one at Bournemouth, one at High Barnet, and one at a place in Dorset called West Moors. Why?"

"I suppose because at some time the place was open common land, lying to the west of some enclosure. . . ."

"I am being very calm, Blow. Try, please, to give me your attention. Why were those mattresses ripped, and by whom. *By whom?*"

"Yes, yes, I see that it is very mysterious. But, Manciple, the thing is a matter for the police, not for you. You have work of your own, my dear fellow. Don't be sidetracked at your time of life."

"Miss Fisk is the one. I feel assured of it. The minister of St. Bede's, whom I met yesterday on the esplanade, says she joined his flock—that was his own word, Blow, not mine—about ten months ago, bringing a letter of introduction from the minister at West Moors in Dorset. Not only that; he tells me that in conversation with her he has often heard of the happy time she had while living in Bournemouth."

"I could never be happy there, I fear. The service to Oxford is impossible."

"It seems to have suited Miss Fisk. And one thing more. Miss Fisk wears an ornament of china or enameled tin carrying the arms of Arundel and an inscription which says 'Good Luck from Arundel.' I have seen it pinned to the front of her clothes."

"That proves no personal connection with the town. Miss Fisk is the kind of person who makes purchases for personal adornment at jumble sales and bazaars."

"I agree, Blow. All the same, it is suggestive. I think we ought to question the lady discreetly. Why don't you ask her to tea?"

"I shall certainly do nothing of the kind. *You* ask her."

"Your flat is on a level with hers, but mine is one floor below. Even the talents of Miss Fisk, I think, do not run to crawling face downward down the wall, like a second Count Dracula."

71

"I can never understand how you find time to read sensational fiction, Manciple. I have difficulty in keeping up with essential reading myself."

"It is true there is a work called, I think, *Dracula*. But I derive my knowledge of the story from a visit to the cinema. I suppose when he crawls down the castle wall they photograph it flat and then turn the picture sideways."

"Unless he crawls up the wall, and they simply reverse it. But I confess the subject seems to me hardly one for intelligent conversation. Nor do I wish to take tea with Miss Fisk."

"Then you'd better go out this afternoon from half-past four until a quarter to six. I have already asked the lady to attend; and I have given your housekeeper half a crown to buy comfits. I am quite willing to share in the expense."

"Then I have only this to say, Manciple. Please go home until half-past four and leave me to my work. I say, Manciple, do you think she used the same knife every time? That would be very suggestive."

"Of what?"

"Of a settled habit. No one doing such a thing on impulse would always find a suitable knife ready to hand. We must contrive an occasion to examine the contents of her reticule. I am getting quite excited at this prospect of the chase! *Hudibras* is sometimes a little humdrum, do you know."

"Never read it, to be frank. Waiting for your edition, Blow. That's loyalty, eh, old fellow? And now I'm off."

"It must be all of twenty years since I had a lady to tea," Dr. Blow told himself after the Professor had gone. "Dear me! I wonder if Miss Angell will give us muffins."

The Chief Constable listened carefully to Inspector Urry's progress report. It was not a very long one, because there had, in fact, been no particular progress, although there had been a great deal of miscellaneous police activity. Everybody living within range of Dr. Blow had been interrogated about their knowledge of Mrs. Sollihull and on other points of possible use. Five people who had actually spoken to Mrs. Sollihull during the fortnight of her employment with the Doctor had repeated their conversations with her in great detail and with great relish. Three of these conversations concerned directions she had asked for in finding her way about a strange town, one resolved itself into a mere exchange of good mornings, and the last may be given verbatim as the witness gave it to the Inspector. "I passed her on the stairs and she said, 'Excuse me.' 'Yes,' I said. She said, 'You look a kind person; can you tell me how to toast cheese, because it keeps falling off the fork.' So I said, 'You put it under the griller.' 'Like a chop?' says she; and I replied, 'Like a chop, unless you fry chops.' 'No,' she says, 'I don't like them fried.' And she went on her way, and I went mine. Next morning she was dead."

"And what does that suggest to you, Inspector?"

"It suggests that she was going to give the Doctor toasted cheese. But he says she never gave him anything. And he'd be sure to remember a thing like toasted cheese."

"Do you think it may mean she was not very experienced in housekeeping? And if that's the case, it can't have been Flash Elsie."

"Of course it was Flash Elsie, sir. Indubitably identified by a hundred little signs, and by fingerprints, come to that."

"Flash Elsie was an expert cook, if she was nothing else."

"Yes. But suppose she was trying to throw somebody off the scent?"

"And whom, pray, might she be wanting to throw off the scent, and off what scent? She was perfectly safe there, and she knew it."

"You haven't noticed, sir, of whom she asked the question. It was Miss Fisk."

"But we are told she and Miss Fisk were on the best of terms."

"Yes. *Miss Fisk told us.*"

"You think Flash Elsie was afraid of Miss Fisk?"

"I don't know, sir. But suppose Miss Fisk was afraid of Flash Elsie? Where does that put us?"

"Urry, come out into the open. Whom do you suspect?"

"I have four suspects at present, sir. 'The Greek,' who is altogether too familiar with the name of Cuttle to suit me. And what has he done with his knife? All seamen carry a knife. Then there's the fellow Alf at the Greek Street Agency; he's obviously in love with Emily Cakebread, and if anything came of that he'd need to be shot of Flash Elsie first. Only I happen to know he was in the cells at Savile Row that night, drunk as a lord. Still, it's all a matter of timing. . . . Then there's Dr. Blow, you know. Looks harmless, but you never can tell; and he once tarred and feathered a statue of Edward the Confessor, which shows a potential of initiative and violence. Alf had motive and Blow had opportunity."

"And 'The Greek' had the weapon. Don't tell me they were all in it together, Urry. That's more than I can swallow."

"No, sir. And indeed I don't very seriously suspect any of them. I'm following up this Miss Fisk. The choirmaster at St. Bede's denies that he ever said she had one of the finest untrained contralto voices he ever heard. That's suggestive, isn't it?"

"But why should the choirmaster of St. Bede's murder Flash Elsie?"

"Not that, sir. Why should Miss Fisk say he said her voice was jolly good, when it isn't. Vanity, sir, self-delusion. And when a woman gets like that, anything can happen. Suppose Elsie said, casual-like, 'Yes, borrow the nutmeg by all means, but for heaven's sake stop singing the Hallelujah chorus through my bedroom wall,' wouldn't that sign her death warrant?"

"I doubt it," said the Chief Constable, "but I don't want to pour cold water on your hopes. By all means get after Miss Fisk. I suppose that *is* the right way to toast cheese, Urry? We don't want to make fools of ourselves."

Miss Fisk liked going out to tea for several reasons. To begin with, she was a gregarious soul, and then every mouthful taken at the expense of another was a positive gain to her precarious finances. Miss Fisk was a gentlewoman, but distressed; so distressed, indeed, that she had more than once wondered if Cakebread's could find her employment as a governess or lady companion, but she had never quite fallen so low in spirit as to take the necessary steps. She would remind herself, desperately, that there was still a little hope without that. And, finally, she liked going out to tea because she liked seeing inside other people's houses and flats. It was better than "Now on View"—although that was exciting, too—because things were not bundled up and tied with string.

So Miss Fisk got a piece of blank cardboard out of the Shredded Wheat packet and wrote in crayon upon it: "Gone to tea with Dr. Blow next door if Urgent," and this she propped up against the front door of her flat by the empty half-pint milk bottle. Then she put on her wooden beads and the extra woolies she always wore when visiting, because people had such drafty houses, and then she went carefully round to make sure there was no tap dripping and no gas turned on.

Finally, Miss Fisk walked down the stairs and out into the street and in at the front door of Dr. Blow's house next door and up the stairs to the front door of his flat. Miss Fisk understood etiquette of this sort perfectly. If you went out to tea by invitation, you never went over the roof.

10

Dr. Blow's study was somehow different, Professor Maniciple thought. And then he realized that for the first time in twenty years or so the top of the writing table was clear. And there was a bunch of everlasting flowers on it in a delicately traced silver vase. These usually stood, as the Professor well knew, on a corner bracket in the hall over the daguerreotype of the Doctor's grandfather, the editor of Steele. Other refinements included an extra chair, both bars of the electric fire switched on, and a strong smell of lavender floor polish. Dr. Blow was wearing a suit Maniciple had never seen before, and within a yard of him, all round, the lavender smell competed with a powerful odor of moth balls. Maniciple himself had risen to the occasion by wearing the ribbon of an obscure Greek Order, which he had received for his paper on the coinage of Troy.

But all these preparations were as nothing beside Miss Fisk's violet lipstick, especially as a large smear of it on her forefinger was gradually communicating traces of itself to everything she touched. She had shaken hands with the two old gentlemen, and had got some on her muffin and some on her nose. The item was advertised as proof against all wear and tear, including the assaults of passion, but it remained to be seen if the Doctor would be able to get it off his copy of Samuel Butler's *Remains* (1749).

Miss Fisk, like many ladies, had perfected the knack of making a hearty tea without being deprived of a lion's share of the talking.

"Well, perhaps just half a cup more," she was saying, "so as to help down this really excellent muffin. Gentlemen do seem to serve the best muffins, I always say, not that I go out to tea with gentlemen very often, you must really not think that! But the minister is very fond of them. And now, to change the subject—for my mother always said, never overpraise the food, that is just as ill-bred as not to express any appreciation at all—thank you, perhaps one lump—I must tell you how splendid I thought you at the inquest, dear Dr. Blow. And how distinguished he looked, Professor. It must have made the coroner very conscious of his pimples."

"Pimples are embarrassing in a coroner, I suppose. But I didn't see you at the inquest, Miss Fisk."

"When the police told me I should not be required to give evidence I feared I should not be able to get in, but that young policeman who had nosebleed and gave me such a fright got me in. It was so strange to think that last time we met I held a saucepan lid under his nose—almost an act of intimacy!"

"An office, I think, rather than something more familiar," Dr. Blow observed. "An impersonal act, whereas anything properly describable as intimate presupposes some emotional commitment. But these are waters in which we are all unaccustomed voyagers, eh, Manciple?"

"You must not speak for Miss Fisk," said the Professor waggishly. He went slightly pink.

"I thought the coroner was very rude," Blow remarked. " 'Just answer my question,' he kept on saying, almost as though I were engaging him in irrelevancies. I'm sure I am quite as busy as he, and with as little time to waste."

"I think he saw no obvious connection between the body of Mrs. Sollihull and the poems of Samuel Butler," Miss Fisk suggested.

"Probably not, which is all the more reason why he should have allowed me to complete the quotation. The appositeness of any allusion depends upon a clear context. Consider further his foolish insistence on my calling Mrs. Sollihull 'the deceased Cuttle.' It confused me, I confess, whereas the purpose of eliciting evidence is to clarify and not to obscure."

"I thought you spoke with dignity and address."

"I was certainly discreet. If I had foolishly blurted out all Manciple and I have discovered . . ."

"Blow, my dear fellow, discretion is laudable at all times. Miss Fisk may feel a delicacy at sharing our secrets."

"Oh, no! dear Professor. I am also most discreet. I am as secret as the grave, all my friends say."

"Just so. Well, Miss Fisk, I think Dr. Blow will not object if I tell you one thing: *We are on to the business of the mattresses.*"

"I am very much afraid I am unable to follow you, Professor Manciple."

"Ha!" said Dr. Blow, "but we have been following you, dear lady, from Arundel to High Barnet, from Fowey to West Moors!"

"Although this impertinence is on a par with using margarine on muffins—and I set both down to your inexperience in polite usages—I must say, Dr. Blow, that I find your behavior extraordinary. From Arundel to High Barnet, indeed, I presume you allude to my occasional residences in these places. And why not? I suppose next you will be accusing me of occupying a basement suite in the Mile End Road. I lived with most respectable people, and kept myself to myself, and am a responsible person free to live where I choose and without reference to either of you gentlemen."

"Really, Manciple, I believe Miss Fisk is right, you know."

"You are easily swayed, Blow. Give her another half-cup of tea, then. But I shall ask just this: Miss Fisk, why did you happen to mention the Mile End Road?"

"I just happened to mention it, in order to say—and I admit with a tinge of un-Christian sarcasm—that I had never lived there. It was by way almost of raillery."

"You have never lived there?"

"Certainly not. I don't even know where it is. I just happen to have seen the address on a pickle jar, that's all."

"You have never lived there. But let me tell you somebody who has: *Flash Elsie,* at eight hundred and fourteen B. That's the basement flat."

"Thank you, most interesting," said Miss Fisk. "I suppose you are suggesting that now the lady is dead, the flat is to let? But I have no wish to reside in the Mile End Road, even in a basement flat at eight hundred and fourteen B."

"It is rather a remote and inaccessible address," Dr. Blow put in. "Practically the same as living at somewhere like Upminster. Such an unlikely place for General Oglethorpe to be buried, I always think."

"Eight hundred and fourteen B," said Miss Fisk under her breath. She always preferred to write things down, but to do so on this occasion would certainly invite comment. Dr. Blow she could deal with, but this Professor Manciple seemed to be another matter. At least, they could have nothing definite. There were no fingerprints.

Professor Manciple was speaking again, firmly but kindly. "Miss Fisk," he said, "it is today increasingly difficult for a single gentlewoman to live. The Doctor and I greatly admire your ability in this particular. You must have shrewd investments."

"Well, I knit most of my things, you know. And, of course, I can play the organ occasionally at weddings; and people are very kind. And, if we are to be so frank with one another, perhaps Dr. Blow will tell us what there is these days in editing the classics."

"It varies, my dear lady, but I am lucky enough to have something in the bank. One must never expect such a poet as Cowley to become what is loosely called a 'bestseller'; but I believe Wiggs of Jesus did very well with his *Decameron*."

"We had better be honest with Miss Fisk," Manciple said abruptly. "Miss Fisk, we know—I say, we *know*—that you didn't come into this flat that night to make toast for your supper. No single gentlewoman dines twice. A witness has come forward who smelt baked beans in your apartment earlier that evening, and the empty tin was found corroboratively in your ash can when you put it out. You admitted a preoccupation with the late Mrs. Sollihull's watch, and I want to know why. Mrs. Sollihull was murdered, let me remind you, and her watch is missing."

"Exactly. And it wants to be found. Her people are entitled to it."

"That's very true," Blow interposed. "Nobody has come forward yet to claim her effects."

"Don't tell me you were acting on behalf of her people!"

"Every one of us has a duty to do what seems right," Miss Fisk said.

"Surely it can never be right to rip open somebody else's feather mattress?"

"If I had murdered Mrs. Sollihull—and I hardly knew her— it would have been quite unnecessary for me to come in looking for her watch. That much is obvious. Furthermore, I already have a watch; here it is. Dear me, it is positively ten to six. I must go, dear Doctor, if I am to hear the news. This has been a most pleasant occasion for me, even though I have once or twice felt that Professor Manciple was verging on the impertinent. I am luckily able to deal with liberties; we women quickly learn that."

"Our sole interest is in establishing the truth," the Professor assured her. "Nothing personal. You will agree that it is a suspicious circumstance, when people go out making surreptitious toast and haven't brought the butter."

"Pooh," said Miss Fisk, "everyone knows you don't put butter on if you're going to dip it in your Bovril."

"The lady has an answer for everything," Dr. Blow remarked, after Miss Fisk had gone. "But I can't help wondering if they are the right answers. She seemed very cheerful when she left; she was humming a hymn, but she can't have been timing an egg."

"No," said Professor Manciple, "she was memorizing an address. It was the baritone air of hymn eight hundred and fourteen. Miss Fisk isn't the only one that was brought up Chapel."

"What a curious way to remember things," said Dr. Blow. "I always write them down." But he began tentatively to hum a garbled rendering of "For All the Saints."

Professor Manciple settled quietly back in his chair again—he had no wish to go home and hear the news—and when the Doctor had come to the end of his music the Professor said softly, "What's the betting, Blow, that there are wild events tonight in the Mile End Road?"

"Did this lady, Flash Elsie, really live there?"

"You were at the inquest; didn't you hear the evidence?"

"Oh, well, if it was mentioned at the inquest Miss Fisk was entitled to hear it, too. She was there."

"I know she was there. So why did she say she got it off a pickle jar, which is one of the most casual ways of getting any address. She said it because she didn't want me to know she had understood its significance."

"Well, and what is its significance?"

"Cast your mind back. First there was evidence of identity— you said it was your housekeeper, and the police said they recognized her as one Flash Elsie Cuttle. Then, very naturally, the coroner said who was Flash Elsie, and everyone craned forward."

"Yes, I remember craning forward."

"And the Superintendent said Flash Elsie was a thief who posed as a housekeeper and took the chance to steal the silver and any other portable valuables before disappearing."

"I thought it very unlikely, because how would she have got those really excellent references?"

"Forged, of course. They stick at nothing. Well, then he went on to describe her previous convictions and so on. And did you notice this, she had been caught, or at least suspected, in cases of silver-stealing at Barnet, Arundel, West Moors, Bournemouth, and Fowey."

"Yes, well, there's still quite a lot of silver about, you know."

"Considerably less, I fancy, after the late Mrs. Cuttle had passed by. Now, I've been checking on this. Those cases were all roughly co-incident with the mattress outrages of which we have record. What do you say to that?"

"Highly ingenious, Manciple."

"I think she hid the stuff in her mattress every time, and this Miss Fisk used to follow up and collect it after Flash Elsie had gone. You see the beauty of it? Flash Elsie disappears and the hue and cry after the silver goes with her. Then little Miss Fisk comes timidly along on pretense of borrowing a pinch of fuller's earth, and collects the swag."

"Why didn't this Elsie take it with her?"

"Domestics are not in the habit of leaving their place of employment carrying heavy bags of stolen property; she might have met her mistress on the stairs, or anything. But Miss Fisk, in all those woolies, she had no shape anyway. I bet she used to hang the fish knives round her middle and carry the tea service openly in a string bag. She'd make out she was absent-minded, if anybody said anything."

"But she says she hardly knew Mrs. Sollihull."

"Perhaps she didn't; what can it matter now? If we can show that she was in all those towns at the same time that Flash Elsie was there—and the presumption is very strong that she was—then we're halfway to solving this whole unhappy tangle."

"Yes," said Dr. Blow. "We must not lose sight of our objective. It is not, who made off with a handful of silver at High Barnet, but who stabbed my housekeeper in the next room? That's what matters. I have not lost any silver."

"Have you not?" asked Manciple with deep irony.

The everlasting flowers lay in a huddled bunch on the table. Of the silver vase there was no sign.

"I distinguish this from kleptomania," Dr. Blow explained to Inspector Urry, as that worthy sat attentively hearing all about it half an hour later. "After all, kleptomania is occasioned by the excitement. Women are always a little highly strung in big shops. But to say in cold blood, 'Just another half-cup please,' and then pocket a man's ornaments while his back is turned putting in the sugar, that is altogether deliberate. I must formally accuse Miss Fisk of filching my flask—ahem, that appears a pleasantly alliterative piece of phrasing, does it not. I see I am not so upset as I feared. The literary man is often calmer than the soldier or the man of affairs. All the same, I am really at my wit's end to know what to put these everlasting flowers in."

At this moment Miss Angell ushered in Constable Elkins, who saluted the company and stood expectant of permission to speak.

"All right, Elkins." The Inspector nodded. "These gentlemen know all about it. Let's hear the story."

"At twenty minutes to seven, sir, on instructions from Sergeant Edge, I proceeded to the premises occupied by Miss Ellen Fisk and knocked on the door. There was no answer. Propped against her door was a notice which said, 'Gone to tea with Dr. Blow next door if Urgent.' So I came here, because police business is always urgent." He looked round the room, as if searching for Miss Fisk.

"She's gone; and gone, too, is an antique silver vase, the property of Dr. Blow," the Inspector explained. "Now what do we do?"

"Comb the pawnshops, sir."

Blow and Manciple exchanged glances, but said nothing. Blow shoved the catalogue of the Army & Navy Stores a little further out of sight among a pile of bound copies of the *Transactions* of the Royal Society of Literature. Manciple began mentally working out which train she must have caught.

"I wonder," said Inspector Urry. "Well, Elkins, you can try. But I think the key to this business lies elsewhere." He turned abruptly to Professor Manciple and said, "There's a seaman down at the harbor called 'The Greek.' He seems to have lost his sheath knife, but he went to the pictures on the Tuesday night. It's always good to have an alibi, Professor."

"I occasionally go to the pictures myself."

"He saw a film called—*Dracula*," began Dr. Blow.

"Excuse me, sir. I want to finish telling Professor Manciple about 'The Greek.' Sometimes he ships in a coaster, but usually he serves in tramp steamers trading in the Mediterranean or up to Riga and Archangel. So he's away from home most of the time. When he is at home, and when he isn't at the pictures, do you know where he can usually be found?"

"Eight hundred and fourteen B Mile End Road," said the Professor.

"Check," said Inspector Urry.

11

Dr. Blow had insisted on wearing a cap, which he had pulled down over his ears in a manner similar to Irving's in a play called *The Dead Heart.* The Doctor had not taken it into account that a melodrama based on the French Revolution could hardly inspire an effective disguise for use in the Mile End Road. However, it was a wet night, and nobody took much notice of the two friends as they crouched in the dark doorway of an empty shop and peered across at number eight hundred and fourteen. They could see little of the basement, which was almost wholly underground at the front of the house (although possibly it opened into a yard at the back). A grating, partly in the pavement, revealed below it a grimy front window; no light gleamed behind the drab drawn curtains. It was after eleven o'clock.

Manciple had acted with resolution. As soon as they had hurried the Inspector off, he had telephoned for a cab and got Blow to the station almost before the Doctor realized that they were on their way once more. The train journey had taken the usual hour, and from Victoria they had traveled by District Line to Liverpool Street and thence by bus to the Mile End Road.

"She had barely an hour's start of us," the Professor had pointed out, "and she probably stopped on the way for a cup of tea or something. And she may indeed have gone to Greek Street, though I doubt if she'd risk that, not at night. No place for a woman, that."

"I've heard—this is pure hearsay, Gideon—that Soho swarms with women at night."

"Not Miss Fisk's sort."

"Oh, really! How is one to tell? After all, we have neither of us known the lady for more than a few days, and already we have learned that she is implicated in theft and murder, despite an obviously careful upbringing. What other misdemeanors may lie at her door?"

"Perhaps there is something in what you say. At all events, we are here to try to find out. And I fancy we shall learn shortly— isn't that Miss Fisk now?"

"Miss Fisk and friend, I fancy. A change for Miss Fisk to be the principal figure in the picture, eh?"

Two people were coming along on the other side of the road, obviously walking from the bus stop at the corner from which, a moment since, a bus had pulled away. Miss Fisk was clearly identifiable, for even in the Mile End Road a knitted overcoat excites remark. Beside her walked a more conventional figure in belted raincoat and trilby hat, looking uncommonly like Alf. They spoke little, and hurried anxiously along, diving into the narrow entrance of the house without a backward glance; which was just as well, for Dr. Blow had scuttled across the road crab-wise and was now crouching scantily concealed by a letterbox, barely six yards away. The two people in the house could be heard clumping down uncarpeted basement stairs for a moment, then a brief silence, then a gas jet began to hiss and a faint blue light gleamed through the curtains.

"Now what?" asked Manciple, joining his friend. "Was it they?"

"Indubitably," Blow replied. "And not only that; they were obviously well known to one another, and to the house. They went in without hesitation and I daresay they're making tea down there now."

"You have a longer neck than I, see if you can squint through the blind."

Supported by the Professor, and heedless of what might be thought by any passer-by, Dr. Blow leaned his head through the gap in the grating between the pavement edge and the wall of the house, and brought his eye and nose up against the grimy glass just where there was the merest crack in the curtain. And then he gave a little scandalized exclamation and hastily withdrew, scraping the skin off his nose in the process.

"I'm very much afraid it is not tea they are making," he said, his cheeks pink. "Indeed, no. They are making love."

"Good," said Manciple, cheerfully, "that is sure to take a little time. And I dare say they'll make tea afterward. Our best move is to go up to the West End and pay a visit to Greek Street. That young man Jim is sure to have got a situation by now, and if not, he'll have gone to the pictures. It's a bit of luck finding Alf and Miss Fisk together and so busy about their own affairs."

"You take it very well," Dr. Blow remarked, "in view of your own predisposition in Miss Fisk's favor."

"Rubbish, William. I've told you before. My interest in Miss Fisk is entirely professional, if I may phrase it so. I mean, I am interested in her as a part of my detecting activities; nothing to do, of course, with numismatics—though, indeed, now I think of it, there are certain cash of the Yuan dynasty which bear images uncommonly like . . . But those are in fact dragons, and one must not be ungallant."

"Then we may leave Alf to his affairs and pursue our own. I think I see a bus now which will take us to Liverpool Street."

The Doctor never felt quite at home in London these days. He missed the hansom cabs, for one thing, and for another, he had difficulty in recognizing policemen, now that they wore collars and ties. However, the present journey was easy enough—bus to Liverpool Street, train to Tottenham Court Road, and then the walk across quiet Soho Square and into Greek Street.

Manciple had expected to find the premises deserted, but in this he was disappointed. All the upper floors were dark, it was true. But the basement was lit, though dimly, and what was worse, there came from under the street the sound of music.

"Dear me," said Blow, "I hope that young man is not entertaining guests in the furnace room when Alf's back is turned."

"I think not," Manciple pronounced. "It is the other rooms that are lighted. They were naturally deserted when we came before, because, as I now see, they are the premises of a night club."

"A night club!"

"Yes—here is the name: Bamboni's. Members Only. This may be of great moment to us, Blow. It gives us a reason for being in this building at a late hour. We must join the club!"

"Join the club! But my dear Manciple, it is extremely unlikely that the facilities offered will rival those we already enjoy. All that foolish and raucous music! And I should doubt very much if they have anybody at all knowledgeable on the wine committee."

"We are not joining for the wine, nor to sit and read the Manchester *Guardian*, nor yet to work out a problem in chess. This is not that sort of club, Blow. You must be realistic. It is what is known as a dive, a place of resort, you know."

As they stood hesitating at the head of the stairs one of the doors below opened, letting a bar of dim orange light into the grimy passage, and a young girl ran laughing up the stairs, calling over her shoulder, "You and who else . . . ?"

"Whom," said the Doctor instinctively, not with any desire to instruct but merely from a tender regard for the language which is our common heritage.

She saw him for the first time as she drew level, for the ground floor passage was in deep shadow. "Why, hullo!" she said.

"Er, hullo," said Dr. Blow, raising his hat and thus at one stroke restoring to himself the appearance of a sentient being.

Manciple said firmly, "Good evening."

Her smile embraced them both so warmly that the Doctor fell back a step, and it was Manciple who continued the conversation.

"We were attracted by the music," he explained. "So gay, you know! This is a club, isn't it?"

"Yes. Why don't you join . . . and come and buy me a drink! Harry's there; you just pay five shillings—each."

"I am so seldom in London," Dr. Blow began, "and I am already a member of the . . ."

"Nonsense, Blow," Manciple interrupted. "You know perfectly well there is neither music nor charming company at your other club. Just old fogies, my dear."

"I like old fogies," she said, her bold black eyes resting for a moment on Dr. Blow's mild blue ones.

"Come, Blow!" said Manciple, taking the Doctor's arm.

The young lady took the other, and the cavalcade descended the stairs in a huddle of legs and feet. The staircase was very narrow, and the Doctor detected an uncommon something in the air about him, which to his horror he presently identified as the lady's perfume, heady and clinging. But it was too late to withdraw, for already Manciple was writing their names—two names, at all events—in a big book, and handing over a ten-shilling note to the man called Harry, whose crumpled dinner jacket at once identified him as an official. All the other men present wore exotic draped suits and extraordinary accessories. Each of them had a girl perched on his knee or sitting close by him. The room was dim with cigarette smoke, and three men in their shirt sleeves were pounding out strident and unfamiliar music from a piano and two fiddles.

"I'm Laura," their mentor confided, taking Dr. Blow by the hand and leading them toward a dark, unoccupied corner. "Who are you?"

"Freddy," Manciple said quickly. "And I'm Jimmy, aren't I, Fred?"

"Just so," said the Doctor, entering as best he might into the spirit of the thing. "Jimmy, yes. Jimmy of Queen's, you know."

"Queen's?"

"Queen's Road, Bayswater. Hem. What about a drink?"

"Champagne for me," said Laura, turning her innocent smile on the Professor, whom she rightly judged to be the principal in this comedy team of old idiots.

But Manciple has seen too many places like this at the pictures to be deceived easily. He was prepared to play ball—this expression also came into his mind from a similar source—but he meant to keep a clear head. "Certainly, my dear," he said kindly, "an excellent suggestion—for you. Please ask for it. But I shall take a small Perrier water and so will Freddy."

"In heaven's name, what's that?"

"Fire water. Something for which you are much too young."

A dubious bottle was set before them and the Professor parted reluctantly with three pounds. Perrier water was not available, and the old gentlemen were served with two splits of ginger ale. The champagne was of no bottling the Professor had ever heard of—although, as he honestly admitted to himself, this was not a subject he had studied fully—and he strongly suspected the contents to be a pale cider laced with South African brandy. Laura sipped it and smoked a good many cigarettes.

One of her hands rested lightly on Dr. Blow's knee, very much to his discomfort. He was afraid to move lest he embarrass her by the discovery that the knee was not her own; and, accordingly, the whole of his left leg had gone to sleep.

Manciple glanced at his watch; it was almost twelve. Time to begin work!

"My dear," he said, "keep Freddy amused, won't you? I must just run out and make a telephone call."

"Of course," she said. "It's the door opposite."

What might be behind the door opposite Manciple did not pause to discover. He was more interested in getting up the stairs unseen and into the offices of the Greek Street Agency on the top floor. As he had expected, the Agency's outer door was locked, but in a surprisingly perfunctory manner. There was no tight-fitting cylinder lock, but merely a padlock fitted to a hasp and staple. Professor Manciple, who, if he had not been so admirable a detective, would have made an excellent criminal, was in no way at a loss. He had in his pocket a Boy Scout knife with the usual instrument for taking nails out of horses' hooves, and in a very short time, and with surprisingly little noise, he had wrenched the hasp off bodily. The screws came out of the old crumbling wood without splintering it; and a glance sufficed to show that when he left he would be able to drive them back again and probably leave no apparent trace. As he contemplated this feat with complacency he allowed himself to wonder whether, after all, numismatics was his true forte; but this was no time for day dreaming! Nobody could tell what folly Blow might be up to in Bamboni's.

The Professor did not dare switch on the lights, but with great enterprise he turned on a small electric fire which, fortunately, was provided with a long wire; and dragging this with him, he was able to direct a red glow at the various objects in the room. Eyes already accustomed to the meager lighting of Bamboni's Club were quite well able to see by this means, until he ventured too far and a jerk pulled out the plug and plunged him in darkness. Nor was this check all, for in his surprise he set the fire down and then could only find it again at the expense of a badly burned thumb. With an oath based on a vernacular inscription in one of the bawdy houses of Pompeii, the Professor sprang back—and thus stumbled upon the great discovery of the evening. *There were not two rooms in this little suite of offices but three.* This discovery he made by plunging through a secret door in the old paneling—a door which, very luckily, opened inward—and landing on his face in a veritable Aladdin's cave, brilliantly lighted and filled with treasure. He scrambled to his feet, bewildered and amazed.

The place was scarcely bigger than a dressing room, and it was constructed in the recess over the stairwell; it might once have housed a water tank or have been a linen closet. Like some safes and refrigerators, it was fitted with an automatic light switch which operated when the door opened, and by this friendly light the Professor saw shelving neatly fitted from floor to ceiling and stacked with choice silverware, some jewelry, and even one gleaming piece of gold plate. It was an excellent sight to see, if the beholder happened to be an elderly amateur detective with barked shins and a blistered thumb, for it represented success in a hazardous calling and the end of the chase in sight. But, like all unexpected successes, it brought its problems with it. What was to be done next?

Professor Manciple pondered. He could ring up the police, he supposed—the irony of adding this call to the criminals' telephone bill appealed to him. On the other hand, if the police came and found Dr. Blow in any sort of embarrassing situation—and it was likely enough that they would—this might make his relationship with the University Press a little awkward, and Manciple doubted if any other publisher would look kindly on the chance of re-issuing *Hudibras* after a couple of centuries of comparative obscurity. He had, after all, a duty to his old friend.

But if he didn't ring up the police, must he then abandon all this beauty to its fate—and there might indeed be a reward —and wantonly acquiesce in its being melted down and probably used for making counterfeit half-crowns? No, not counterfeit half-crowns, of course, for the whole point of those was that they contained no silver. Silly of him! More likely the metal would be made into ingots to finance the activities of the I.R.A. That would be it—or the Mau-Mau or the Ku Klux Klan. The world was full of illicit organizations, he knew; not so much because they figured largely in the Manchester *Guardian* as because the Professor's extensive reading included many of the works of Sax Rohmer.

A third possibility, he reflected, would be to load the loot into a taxicab and take it away. It would be a simple matter to lodge it in the left-luggage department of some great railway terminus or, indeed, one might rent a locker at one's own club for a few nights—though not, of course—ha ha—at Bomboni's! Really, the thought bordered on the droll!

While these several reflections were occupying Professor Manciple's attention he was surprised and perturbed to hear a footstep on the stairs.

"Throw away that nasty ginger and have some of this," Laura invited, pushing her scarcely tasted champagne glass into Dr. Blow's hand. The girl knew what she was doing, for this was not the first occasion that she had sipped of Bomboni's champagne; and, indeed, she had seen it being bottled in the next room.

The Doctor, denied this intelligence and fearful of causing offense, allowed himself to be persuaded. With an extraordinary expression of distaste and apprehension on his face, he drank. Then he spluttered, politely holding his handkerchief before his face. Then he said distinctly and emphatically, " 'Thou that with ale, or viler liquors, Didst inspire Withers, Pryn, and Vickars. . . .' "

"Don't know any of them," Laura interrupted. "Come on, dear, let's dance."

Several couples were moving about the floor, though they could hardly be said to be dancing. There was no room for that. They were merely swaying with locked, oblivious bodies, and breathing down each other's necks.

Laura leaned across the Doctor, her bare shoulder brushing his cheek, and called to the perspiring pianist, "Give us something old fashioned, Perce."

The battering rhythm ceased, and with barely a pause the musicians began something which might, perhaps, have been a selection from *The Maid of the Mountains;* but although Laura's thoughtfulness had made dancing possible for the Doctor from one point of view, other circumstances conspired to withhold from him this unwonted pleasure. As the Doctor had not yet realized, his left leg had gone to sleep. Accordingly, when he stood up, he, for the first time since Boat Race night, 1897, fell flat on his face.

"That's enough of that!" cried Harry, pushing his way through the throng.

The dancing ceased, and a West Indian girl took the opportunity of erasing a slight crinkle in her stocking and re-fastening her garter, to the prostrate Doctor's fascinated horror.

Laura said briskly, "Better get him over to my place. It's the heat."

"My leg went funny," said the Doctor weakly. He was now on all fours, feeling and looking uncommonly foolish. "If somebody would give me their arm . . ."

"He never got it here," Harry said. He jerked the Doctor upright and said, "It's three pounds for the champagne, six shillings for the ginger ale. And you didn't pay the guinea entrance fee."

"Where is Manciple?" asked Dr. Blow, looking about him in a sudden panic.

"Four pounds seventeen," said Harry. "We don't want your sort here."

"Come along, dear," said Laura, "I'll make you a nice cup of tea."

The club secretary assisted Dr. Blow to get five pounds from his wallet and then took him firmly by the arm. Laura slipped her arm through his on the other side, and the melancholy procession made its way up the stairs, Dr. Blow muttering faintly, " 'Friend, quoth the elephant, you're drunk!' " He gazed wildly at the unfamiliar and clear emptiness of Greek Street, and allowed Laura to guide him into Carlisle Street across the square. Perhaps it would be advisable, he thought, to take a cup of tea.

12

For two or three seconds Professor Manciple held his breath. Then he realized that the longer he held it, the more painful would be the explosion, when at last it had to be released, and he began with infinite caution to allow his breath to escape. How fortunate, he reflected, that he was not a wheezy man.

In the meantime, the newcomer, although stepping cautiously, as people do when they move about deserted premises after midnight, was not taking any extraordinary precautions. The Professor could very distinctly hear the soft footsteps outside; and he then heard a sharp, indrawn hiss of breath as his visitor found the door forced open. He could see nothing, for he had pushed the door of his retreat back into place in order to shut off the light, and although there remained a very slight crack where it was not quite home, this commanded only a dim prospect of the fireplace in the inner office. So far events without were confined to the region of the front door—if you could call anything so pedestrian by the name of an event, for all sounds had ceased abruptly with that little gasp of surprise. Despite an increasing and, indeed, consuming curiosity, Manciple was forced to remain where he was, for the moment he opened the door of his cupboard in order to get out, the place would be flooded with light. He might have taken out the bulb, it is true, but the most astute of private investigators must occasionally be allowed to overlook something, and this practical means of effecting an unobtrusive exit escaped him. Besides, he already had one scorched thumb.

Accordingly, the Professor applied an anxious eye to the crack and waited.

In the outer office a tall, shadowy figure stood perfectly still, irresolute. There was the door, offering a line of retreat. There, on the other hand, lay invitingly open the connecting door giving access to the inner office. Everything was silent, dark. At last, with screwed-up courage, the intruder tiptoed with infinite caution toward the Professor's territory and crossed between him and the fireplace. For a brief moment the Professor was able to see something different from cracked tiles, a black hole, and a gas ring with a tin kettle on it. As the figure crossed his line of vision, even Manciple's limited experience told him that this was a woman.

With a little click she switched on a shaded reading lamp on the desk. There were no blinds, but it was a necessary risk, and the window overlooked only roofs and chimneys, being at the back away from the street. The connecting door between the two main rooms closed.

It was very provoking; the Professor couldn't see a thing beyond the now brightly illuminated tin kettle and its immediate surroundings.

Shuffling noises and the crackle of papers. The sound of breathing.

The sound of a match striking—good heavens, was the woman going to make herself a cup of cocoa?

She came between him and the light and bent at the fireplace. In the shadow he saw the reflection of a tiny, growing flame. She was burning papers.

The Professor had a scholarly instinct against the destruction of the written word, whatever it might be. The ephemera of one age is the source material of the next. What would not Manciple have given to have access even to the waste-paper baskets and dust bins (if it had any) of the Royal Mint at the time of Charles the First! Fire is ever the archivist's enemy.

With an agitated little, "Oh, dear me, no!" Professor Manciple stepped out of his hiding place.

The lady leaped up, cracked her head on the overhanging mantelpiece, gasped inarticulately, and fell like a tree. With a courtesy innate and Old World the Professor caught her, staggered back under the plunging weight, and sat down heavily, allowing the insensible face of Miss Emily Cakebread to bury itself in his shoulder. Under this impact it seemed that the entire building shook, but in the basement two fiddles and one piano continued playing and twenty cramped, oblivious bodies continued to sway on a dance floor eight feet by ten. One beetle was dislodged from the ceiling in the outer office of Gunstein's theatrical agency and landed in a bag of almond fudge. This happened to be the place it was making for anyway.

"Miss Cakebread!" gasped the Professor, as soon as he had gathered sufficient breath.

The lady opened her eyes. "Miss Emily Cakebread," she murmured. "Miss Cakebread is my sister, you know. We are a little alike, but she is by some years the elder." She closed her eyes again.

With a movement born of a mixture of caution and curiosity, the Professor allowed his hand to rest lightly upon Miss Emily Cakebread's hair. Yes, there was a distinct bump, but the injury was obviously of no permanent importance. The blow could hardly have unbalanced even the most delicate reason.

Reassured, the Professor allowed Miss Emily Cakebread's person to slide off his knees to the floor, where he thoughtfully put a copy of *Who's Who,* 1938, under her head. She didn't look comfortable, he conceded, even thus, but the book at least raised her a little from the ignominy of lying flat on her back on a strip of cold lino printed in imitation of Axminster carpet, which would have been the alternative. And if she wanted comfort, she could have stayed at home in her own bed.

Meanwhile, he turned his attention to the fireplace, which had resumed its former inhospitable blackness. A pile of paper ash was all that remained of whatever it was the lady had been burning. Gray against the black, a few words could be seen on one crumpled sheet, and over this the Professor eagerly bent. ". . . ency . . . the Princess . . . Gand . . ." he read. He prodded at the pile and it fell apart. A single corner of paper remained unconsumed, and this the Professor put into his notebook before turning again to his companion. She was sitting up.

"Aren't you going to say 'Where am I'?" asked the Professor with interest. In matters of this sort his extensive reading had taught him what was correct.

"I know very well where I am," Miss Emily Cakebread answered, not without spirit. "This is the office of Cooks and Butlers Limited, the Greek Street Agency, with whom I have long enjoyed close business associations. Not only do I know where I am, but I consider myself fully entitled to be here, although the circumstances are admittedly a little unusual. I doubt whether you can say the same, Professor Gilbert Manciple."

"Gideon."

"If you were a gentleman you would offer me some assistance, instead of standing staring at me. I am injured and I am suffering from shock."

"I have felt your bump, Miss Emily Cakebread, and even my limited medical knowledge suffices to assure me that it is nothing. You have sustained no fracture, no concussion even. If you have so much as a headache, it will be occasioned rather by your continuing to lie in that constrained position than by the original blow. Believe me, madam, you have had a fortunate escape. I was far more gravely injured on my own initial entry into these premises. I have a badly burned thumb, for one thing, and several painful contusions about me. These are a natural part of detective work, and this recalls me to my purpose. Why are you here after midnight destroying evidence? Answer me that!"

"You are not a detective. You are second cousin to Lady Orelebar, and you seem to share the conspicuously domineering nature which distinguishes her family. How dare you cross-question me about my movements! For all you know, I might be a silent partner in the concern, or Alf might have lent me his keys, or anything. It would be more to the point if you explained your own presence."

"Murder brings me here, Miss Emily."

"Don't you threaten me, or I shall scream. I shall say you hit me on the head, and I have the bump to prove it."

"Won't you stand up, please? Rational conversation is impossible between two persons, one of whom is lying prostrate on the floor. I am entirely willing to take you into my confidence, for I believe you to be an innocent party."

Miss Emily Cakebread blushed. "If you felt as ill as I do, you'd be lying on the floor, too. I consider everything you have done and said highly suspicious. I find you here, with the door forced open and everything, and then you talk wildly about detectives and murder. Anybody would think it was you that had received a severe blow on the back of the head. However, if you will be kind enough to give me your arm I will essay to stand up. Is there a mouthful of water in the kettle? Alf has a bottle of aspirin in the top left-hand drawer of his desk."

Manciple helped her to her feet and established her on a chair, moving about thereafter in his ministrations. He poured a little water into a cup and found the aspirins.

"Drink this," he said, employing the classic formula and supporting her with an arm unnecessarily flung about her shoulders.

"You are very good," she said, her mood changing. He was handsome, she reflected. That, at least, was something he did not have in common with his second cousin.

"Now," said Professor Manciple, "you are refreshed and sustained. You are in no danger, I assure you. Murder was never my intention; it was merely the occasion of my presence here. The key to the death of Dr. Blow's Mrs. Sollihull lies somewhere in this office, I am convinced. It was my purpose to find it. And I ask you again, Miss Emily, *why were you burning papers?*"

"Have you never thought that there may be people who do not wish the mystery to be solved?" she questioned him in her turn. For the first time she looked him straight in the eyes. "What was Flash Elsie to you?"

There was a long pause, and then Professor Manciple replied slowly, "And what is Alf Cuttle to you?"

"Cuttle!" she cried, her voice rising to a shriek. "Cuttle! Then I've been double-crossed! He said it was Carter."

Professor Manciple was struck by the animation in her voice, the flash of light in her eye. Really, for a moment he thought her almost beautiful. After all, to a man of sixty-nine, forty-seven seems hardly old. "You were too good for him, my dear," he said softly.

To be stroking a woman's hair at one o'clock in the morning was with Professor Manciple an experience so novel as to be virtually unprecedented. Nonetheless, he found it stimulating. Miss Emily Cakebread's reaction to it could not be conjectured with any accuracy, because she had gone to sleep.

"This is uncommonly pleasant," the Professor murmured to himself, venturing to brush the lady's cheek with his lips, "but it is also uncommonly inconvenient. Emily is obviously overwrought and justly so. But we cannot remain here. It is a compromising situation from almost every point of view, although my intentions are wholly honorable. We are, in a certain sense, housebreakers. We have destroyed evidence—for I must identify myself with dear Emily's actions, I suppose. We are on enclosed premises, with intent. And, I must confess it, the sweet creature is a heavy load to bear."

She was sitting on his knee, her arms about his neck and her head against his shoulder. He hardly cared to allow himself the unwonted luxury of recapitulating to himself the astonishing events of the last hour, which had led him at last to this happy position. It was all too overwhelming and too sudden. His extensive experience in numismatics afforded no close parallel, although certain early Greek coins did, now he came to think of it, bear images calculated to bring to the cheek of awakening love something in the nature of a blush. He must hide those before he led his bride home. . . .

His bride! Oh, come, now. That was going too far and too fast. Even Professor Manciple could not yet work out a suitable speech by which he might ask of Miss Cakebread the boon of her sister's hand. He closed his eyes, the better to apply his mind to this teasing problem; and it was thus, clasped in one another's arms, fast asleep, that the next visitor found them.

13

"There, dear!" said Laura. "Make yourself comfortable. That's the bathroom through there. I'll put the kettle on for a cup of tea." She vanished through another door, closing it behind her, and Dr. Blow was left to his own devices.

The room in which he found himself was at once intimate and impersonal. Intimate, because it contained a double divan bed with cushions scattered over it, pink subdued lighting, heavy curtains pulled tight across the window, and pictures which to Dr. Blow were a source of surprise and embarrassment. Impersonal, because the whole effect was that of a hotel bedroom—except for the pictures. The place had no air of being lived in, and the few private effects that were to be seen—a comb on the dressing table, something frilly thrown over the back of a chair—had the appearance of being the veneer of a personality imposed fleetingly and impermanently. To have sat on the armchair would have involved the Doctor in resting his head back against the thing with frills. To have sat on the other chair would have brought him face to face with himself in the dressing-table mirror, and he would have felt foolish thus. So he sat on the edge of the bed.

"That's a good boy!" called Laura, her face appearing momentarily at the door. She had changed her dress, Dr. Blow noted, but had not yet remembered to put on another. He had occasionally been similarly absent-minded himself, but he was interested to notice this tendency in one so young. No doubt she would complete her toilet before bringing in the tea.

As it happened, exactly the same line of thought was in Laura's mind, although she had reached it by a different path. It was almost second nature to her to take off her clothes when she brought a guest in—though, oddly enough, she remained fully dressed when alone—but now, as she arranged cups and teapot on a tray, she was wondering if this guest were quite of the customary order. This might be the rare, the almost unprecedented, case of one from whom revenue was to be had without return. Laura was a generous soul, very willing to give clients her best attention at all times, but, like all high-class tradespeople, she refrained from pressing her wares upon the unresponsive. The only thing was these matters were usually satisfactorily thrashed out before she brought clients home. . . . The kettle was boiling now, and Laura put on a dressing gown and made the tea.

Dr. Blow's only concession to the intimacy of the occasion had been to take off his shoes. His normal habits were sedentary, and a seventeen-hour day spent mainly on his feet had produced a certain discomfort more muscular, he opined, than metatarsal; but, though harmless and ephemeral, irritating. At Laura's picturesque suggestion, he was resting his plates of meat—ha ha—and Laura, the tea tray pushed aside, was indulging in the unwonted luxury of lying on her bed with most of her clothes on. The fact that her dressing gown had fallen open she didn't count, and Dr. Blow was too preoccupied to notice. He was telling her about the wretched last days of Samuel Butler, as noticed by Dryden in a letter to the Earl of Rochester.

"And now, my dear," he concluded, "he lies in an unmarked grave in St. Paul's, Covent Garden, with only the dubious adjacent presence of the bones of Peter Pindar to keep him warm!"

"I used to have a room in King Street, Covent Garden, when I was working in Glasshouse Street," Laura said, "but it was a long way. And now, dear, I shall have to be going home soon."

The Doctor looked startled, as well he might. It was singular enough and really rather extraordinary to be sitting with a girl who was on her bed; but how much more so if the bed turned out to be that of some unknown third party—and he with his shoes off!

"But I thought, . . ." he said, hastily sitting up.

She pulled him back with a little laugh, so that he over-balanced and his face positively brushed against her bare shoulder. "Silly!" she said. "I don't *live* here. I get the all-night bus in Oxford Street at ten to four. My place is at Lewisham."

Dr. Blow said soberly, "My dear, I have no doubt you find me a strange visitor; you must forgive me; I want to do what is proper. I have found your hospitality most stimulating and . . ."

"Three pounds," said Laura, briskly. "And if you want . . ."

"Just so," said the Doctor. "Three pounds."

It crossed his mind that one way and another the evening was proving a bit of an expense. But it also represented a rare increment of experience, and, furthermore, his little discourse on the life of Samuel Butler, necessarily set in elementary terms, had clarified in his mind a point that had been teasing him off and on for several years: If Butler's grave were indeed now unknown, as it indubitably was, might not a clue to its whereabouts be discovered by reference to that of Peter Pindar, who had expressly desired to be buried as close as possible to his hero, the elder poet? Of course, if Pindar's grave also remained unidentified . . . Eh? What was this?

Laura's conscience had been troubling her; after all, three pounds bordered on the excessive for a cup of tea, even if he had taken his shoes off. She was wriggling out of her dressing gown.

Dr. Blow raised a long, pale protesting hand and said, "You are a most fetching lady—the phrase is expressive, though colloquial—but, hem, I am not at all the person best to appreciate your charms. I am, however, deeply sensible . . . just so. *Yo soy perro viejo, y no hay conmigo tus, tus*—what a student of human nature Cervantes was! But naturally you are more of St. Augustine's mind, ha ha! *Da mihi castitatem et continentiam, sed noli modo*—yes. But—οὐ φροντὶς Ἱπποκλείδη." *

---

* For his own benefit, for he lacks Dr. Blow's proficiency in the learned tongues, the author begs to append translations of these several statements. The first is from *Don Quixote:* "I am an old dog, and *tus, tus,* will not do

"Then I might as well put on my dressing gown," Laura said.

"And then I'll walk with you to the bus," said Dr. Blow, "—if I may?"

"You devil!" said Laura playfully.

The Doctor watched with interest as his companion completed the simple duties associated with shutting up shop for the night. She washed up the cups and put them away, carefully smoothed the rumpled bed, and carried onto the landing a tin rubbish pail; opened a window and drew back the curtains; switched off all fires and lights. And then she took the Doctor's hand and led him down the stairs. Behind the street door, on an unobtrusive hook, she hung the key of the flat, to Blow's mild wonderment.

"For my friend Millie," Laura explained, "she has the flat from lunchtime till seven o'clock; and before that Florrie comes in to sweep up. Now—come on—take me to the bus stop!"

On the way to the bus stop Laura chatted pleasantly about trifles, leaving the Doctor free to recall himself to the real business of his presence in the metropolis. "I never gave you my telephone," she said, as they turned out of the square. "It's Museum 68783."

"68783, just so—'The perfect number of the Beast'—you must excuse my inveterate habit of quotation, my dear. I mean no disrespect. Whom should I ask for?"

"Surely by now you know my name?"

"Miss Laura—I wondered if it might be Smith or Montgomery or Waugh."

"It's Mrs. Carter, if you must know."

"Not Carter née *Cuttle?*"

"Here's the bus, dear: I must run. Good-bye!"

The Doctor absently raised his hat and stood looking so long after the bus that a black cat had time to cross sedately from Newman Street and rub against his legs.

for me," which corresponds to the English proverb that an old bird may not be caught with chaff. The second is from the *Confessions* of St. Augustine, and means: "Give me chastity and continency, but do not give it yet," an excellent motto for Dr. Blow's hostess; and the last: "Hippocleides doesn't care" is from Herodotus.

It took Dr. Blow some time to find Bamboni's again, although, in fact, the club premises lay only just across the square. This delay he occasioned for himself by walking past the entrance in deep meditation, and he was almost at the junction with Shaftesbury Avenue before he recalled himself to the enterprise upon which he ought to have been engaged. The chance quotation from his favorite poem had stimulated his thoughts—always at their most alert toward four A.M.—and carried them to a relevant passage in Fevardent's *Irenaeus,* the folio edition of 1765. And then—"Oh, come!" he said to himself. "It would be most ungallant to identify Miss Laura with the Antichrist, even though she turns out to be a Cuttle. Really, the experience had elements of the uncommonly pleasant—hem." He turned and made his way back, peering at the street numbers until a familiar doorway took his eye. This must be it: the Greek Street Agency, Bamboni's, and the rest. But the place was in darkness, no soft music, no lingering perfume on the stairs. Just blackness. But at least the street door was unlocked.

Where could Manciple be? Blow gravely doubted his friend's ability to resist any offer of dissipation, and he had been gone nearly two hours.

The basement stairs were pitch black so the Doctor decided first to mount upward, where at least a little light shone through the grimy staircase windows. Up, up he went, past Gunstein and Gunstein; past S. H. Welsh, Commission Agent; past Mr. Cartland of unknown occupation; and on to the top landing. Just so. The Greek Street Agency's front door was open. Dr. Blow stepped in.

His eyes already well accustomed to the dark, he made his way unerringly across the outer office and pushed open the door of the further room. Ha, yes, there was Manciple; you could tell him by the gleaming, even in that gloom, of his patent-leather boots. But he seemed to be not alone; for although Dr. Blow could only distinguish one pair of feet, he could distinctly see two heads.

"Hem!" he said. "Manciple, my dear fellow. Is that you, Gideon?"

"Oh!" said a female voice. There followed a sort of scuffle, and the group in Alf's armchair disintegrated.

"Adsum!" said the Professor, coming out of a profound slumber and scrambling up in his turn.

The lady said, "It is only Dr. Blow. How you startled us! Let us put on the light." She switched it on, and the three confronted one another.

"Dear me," said Dr. Blow.

"I can easily explain," Miss Emily Cakebread began, hastily, but Professor Manciple interrupted.

"Allow me," he said. "Blow, much has happened. We have taken a great step forward. Our investigation here is virtually complete. It is time to pause and take stock. But there seems not to be another chair; a third, I mean, for Miss Emily will also require one. Certain innocent intimacies which are permissible in private can hardly be indulged in when a third person is present, even though, my dear fellow, I have enjoyed your friendship for sixty years. You apprehend?"

"It is certainly desirable for Miss Emily Cakebread to have a chair, Manciple. At need, I would be very willing to stand. But it crosses my mind that in some sort we are trespassing here, and we may be closely questioned if anyone comes. It is almost morning. Alf, for one, is likely to come at any time now. And, as it happens I believe I am in a position to offer alternative accommodation—ha ha! Pray follow me."

"Wait!" said Manciple. He hastily set the office to rights: made sure the concealed door was shut, scattered the ashes in the grate, put back the bottle of aspirins, restored the electric fire to its place, and, finally, shepherding them out, he drove back the screws that held the hasp and staple, leaving the premises with the superficial appearance of having remained undisturbed.

"Now, forward!" he said, and the party tiptoed down the stairs.

In the street the first flush of morning was to be seen above the grimy trees of Soho Square. It was nearly five o'clock.

Dr. Blow led the way without hesitation to Carlisle Street, and without pausing unhooked Laura's front-door key from its place behind the street door. "Allow me to lead the way," he said, mounting the stairs.

In silence, the others followed.

"There!" said Dr. Blow, flinging open Laura's door and ushering them into the bedroom. "A mere *pied à terre*, I confess, but convenient, convenient."

He hastily removed something frilly from the back of the armchair and pushed it out of sight behind the cushion. He was inwardly interested to notice that the object no longer disturbed him; after all, had he not seen such things in domestic use, and not so long since? How soft it was, and dainty! Just so.

"Florrie comes in to sweep up," said Dr. Blow, "but hardly so early as this, I feel sure. Let us be at ease. Pray sit down. Hem! You will excuse me if I sit on the bed and leave you the chairs." He took his shoes off.

Professor Manciple said, "Where shall we begin, Blow, hey? You or me? I think perhaps some parts of your activities are not of a nature for discussion just now. . . ."

"At least I am alone," Blow pointed out. "If I may say so, it seems to me that your own affairs have taken a surprising turn. I have not yet had the honor of an explanation of Miss Emily Cakebread's presence among us."

"I will tell you," said the Professor, and he gave an accurate but not strictly complete recital of the events of the earlier hours. The concealed cupboard he did not mention, nor certain exchanges which in our own narrative we have preferred not to detail at length. The Doctor was quick to pounce on the essentials.

"Destroying what?" he asked accusingly.

Miss Emily Cakebread remained obstinately silent.

The Professor said soothingly, "I feel sure there is a reasonable explanation, Blow. Miss Emily will come to feel a confidence in us; I am sure of it. She will give us every attention and help, I know. But we must not, of course, require her to incriminate herself; no."

"I've done nothing," Miss Emily Cakebread said indignantly. "It was you who broke in, remember that. I've known Alf for nearly twenty years."

"That's nothing," Manciple reminded her, "you didn't know

him very well. Called him Carter, Blow."

"Carter!" said Blow, sitting up. "That reminds me . . . er, nothing. Shall we have a cup of tea?"

"I should like nothing better," Manciple said.

The lady nodded and her face brightened.

Dr. Blow moved familiarly to the door and disappeared; he rather enjoyed doing the honors, and he was not disinclined to suppose the former payment of three pounds sufficient to cover this further incursion. After all, it was by no means time yet for Millie to take over. Ah! Millie—probably she was the proprietor of that wisp of nylon! Just so. He must remember to put it back before leaving. It might not occur to her to look under the cushion.

Left to themselves, Manciple and Miss Emily began to talk in low tones. The Professor had thoughtfully taken Blow's place on the bed; like his friend, he felt foolish sitting at a dressing table. This change in position brought him directly in front of one of Laura's more surprising pieces of art, hanging on the wall above Miss Emily's head. His answers to her remarks became a thought perfunctory; his gaze withdrew itself from hers and wandered away. Gradually, something most curious began to make itself clear to him; this was not a mere provocative photograph torn from some French journal and stuck in a frame. It was a real person, someone he knew. Naturally, he had not recognized her without her clothes on, of course not; no. But those bold eyes, that full lip, the abundant, glossy hair—they could only belong, he opined, to the departed, the unlamented, the disturbing Mrs. Hoptroft!

Mrs. Hoptroft! Was Blow, then, maintaining an illicit liaison? That plausible familiarity with the place for the key! That easy offer of cups of tea, without first looking to see if there were any milk! Those shoes, carelessly left at the side of the bed! Well!

These reflections were interrupted by the return of Dr. Blow carrying a tea tray, which he set down on the dressing table at Miss Emily Cakebread's elbow. "Will you be Mother?" he said, playfully.

Miss Emily blushed, and Manciple said sharply, "Blow, your conversation borders on the wanton! This lady and I . . ."

"Is anybody hungry," Blow interrupted. "A buttered biscuit, hey?"

"I wouldn't say no," said Miss Emily.

"I'll see what I can find," said Dr. Blow. He returned to the little kitchen and began rummaging in cupboards. A tin yielded a handful of dry biscuits, but where was the butter? Salt, jam, corn flakes, fish paste—quite a little store of eatables of one sort and another—but no butter—ah, naturally, it would be in the refrigerator. There was a small refrigerator in the corner and Dr. Blow opened the door; then . . .

"Manciple!" he called softly. "Manciple!"

The Professor answered. "Coming!" He came hurrying in.

By now Dr. Blow had lifted the dish of butter out and put it on the table. There was a pretty big pat—all of half a pound—and the last person to use it had thoughtfully left the butter knife sticking upright in it. Only it wasn't a butter knife, in any ordinary sense of the word.

It was a broad-bladed sailor's knife.

14

The Chief Constable entered his office briskly and sat down at his desk. It was just after ten o'clock, and he meant to deal with his mail before the mid-morning cup of tea came. After that, there was to be a conference; the Chief Constable disliked conferences because people always waited for him to begin, and he could never think of anything to say. "Now then," he would start, "let's begin. All here? Good. Er . . ." And then he'd dry up and everyone would look at him. It was because of this unfortunate inarticulateness that the Chief Constable had taken up smoking a pipe—which he disliked very much. He found that busyness with a pipe often covered up an awkward pause; and a speech punctuated with puff, puff sounded uncommonly impressive. It did to the Chief Constable, anyway.

The mail as usual was meager and dull. A letter threatening what would happen if they didn't leave Micky the Elk alone, unsigned. The usual communication from a Pools promoter who persisted in calling the Chief Constable "M.P.," when any fool knew it ought to be "M.C." Four official letters about minor administrative matters. A magazine devoted to model railways. An advertisement for somebody's patent handcuffs, "the only instrument to balk the great Houdini." And, of course, the *Police Gazette*.

The Chief Constable began to read an article about scale models of broad-gauge locomotives.

All too soon it was conference time. A cold mug of tea stood at his elbow, and the railway magazine lay face down beside it. The Chief Constable pressed his buzzer, and when nothing happened, went to the door and shouted, "Abner!"

A tall thin constable appeared in his shirt sleeves. "Conference!" said the Chief Constable, ignoring the fact that the man's face was lathered all down one side. Recruits were hard enough to get these days, and at least the fellow was clean, half-clean anyhow.

" 'Morning, sir!"

" 'Morning, Urry."

"Good morning, sir. Good morning, Inspector."

" 'Morning, Wix."

" 'Morning, Wix."

"Come in, Elkins. Don't stand there shuffling your feet."

"Yessir. Nosir."

"Well, sit down, all of you. Now then. Let's begin. All here? Good. Er . . ."

A little silence. The scraping of a match. Then, "Well, Urry, eh—puff, puff—what's new?"

Inspector Urry coughed and then said, soberly, "New, sir? Not a thing, if by new you also mean relevant. Plenty that's new, so far as it goes. Detailed case histories from birth to present day on half the inhabitants of this town, but not a line on which of them knifed Flash Elsie. Nor have we found the knife they did it with. We know where the sheath is—if it's the right sheath. We also know pretty fully the plot of a film called *Rock 'n' Roll Blues*. We know further that Dr. Blow has had a silver flower vase nicked from under his very nose; and that Miss Fisk went up to London yesterday afternoon latish and hasn't been heard of since, and so did Manciple and Blow and Miss Emily Cakebread."

"Were they tailed?"

"Not to say tailed, sir. I've only got two men. Elkins was going round the pawnshops; and Sergeant Wix was wanted yesterday afternoon to give evidence about those two boys that broke into the empty house in Worthing Road and stole two flower pots, one garden rake, and a tin of slug detergent. So I had to manage without him all the afternoon. I couldn't tail four people who all went off in different directions."

"Surely Blow and Manciple went together."

"Well, in a manner of speaking, sir, they did. But I also had to keep an eye on the sailor Cuttle, 'The Greek,' as they call him; and I had an interview with Miss Cakebread—the old 'un—and then there was my report in triplicate. . . ."

"Yes, yes, Urry, I know you are short-handed. But you can't expect another penny on the rates every time there's a murder. You could have borrowed a man from point duty—hardly any cars pass Hangman's Corner between two and five—or Abner was here."

"Last time I borrowed Abner, sir, was when those smugglers got away by telling him they were suffragan bishops going on an all-night fishing trip."

"Well, I'd better ask the Yard . . ."

"Oh, sir!"

"Well . . . haven't you got *anything*?"

"On the night of the murder, sir, Miss Emily Cakebread's bed *was not slept in*."

"Come, that's a beginning, Urry. Very good, man! Who told you?"

"Her sister."

"Indeed. And what else did she tell you?"

"Nothing, sir, nothing material that is. A lot of stuff about the Princess Sophey of Gand, which I'd better not repeat. And a great deal of stuff which boils down to nothing at all, like the conversation of most elderly ladies. And this about Emily's bed. She said, 'I am profoundly disturbed, Inspector, that you have allowed a murderer to remain free among us. To think that only last Tuesday we might all have been stabbed in our beds besides that unfortunate Mrs. Carter; except Emily, of course.'

" 'And why except Emily, Miss Cakebread?' I asked.

" 'Because on Tuesday last, Inspector, without mentioning it to me, Emily thought fit not to sleep in her bed. I am profoundly disturbed.'

"So I said, 'Perhaps she had toothache,' and Miss Cakebread said, nastily, I thought, 'She hasn't a tooth in her head.' "

"What's all this worth, Urry?"

The telephone rang and the Chief Constable snatched it up. "I'm in conference," he growled. "Eh? Oh. Wait, then. Urry, it's for you; it's that Miss Cakebread."

The Inspector took the telephone and said, "Yes? Inspector Urry here."

A thin, precise voice came over the wire, loud enough for them all to hear. "Inspector Urry," it said, "my sister Emily's bed has not been slept in again."

"I'll look into it," the Inspector promised, and after a few exchanges he rang off. "Though I don't see any point in looking into it if she isn't there," he added.

"Earache's another thing that sometimes keeps people awake," said Sergeant Wix.

The threat to call in Scotland Yard had upset Inspector Urry. He felt certain the clue to the whole business must be lying at hand; and, in any case, the Yard probably didn't care. They had no cause to love Flash Elsie. Urry pored over the reports again, certain that somewhere he would get a lead; and, sure enough, he did. "Elkins!" he called. "Elkins!"

The Detective Constable came in.

"Elkins, that night you had nosebleed—I've got your report here. You say it came on while Professor Manciple was frying bacon and you did your best to control it. Then, when he had gone, you lay down and closed your eyes. Then you heard Dr. Blow come in and eat his bacon. Then he went away, and after a moment or two someone else came in and bent over you and then screamed; that was Miss Fisk. Then they put you on a stretcher and carried you away. Right?"

"Yessir."

"Four days later you put in an expense voucher for dry cleaning your uniform where it had blood on."

"Yessir, in the course of duty; you said it would be all right up to six shillings."

"Yes, yes, Elkins, I know. *But which of those three people wiped a large bloody knife on the tail of your coat?*"

"Oh, sir, I never knew any of them . . ."

"Take it off."

The Constable removed his coat.

"You paid for cleaning, but you didn't ask for any mending. So here, lo and behold, we find a gash six inches long in the lining. I suppose even your peculiar talents don't run to nose-bleeding down the back of your neck?"

"No, sir. It's cut all right, like as if somebody had wiped a sharp knife. 'Ere, that was a bit of a nerve! I take a poor view of that."

"It's lucky for you you never opened your eyes or you might have had it in your heart, Elkins. Now, it was one of those three. Which? Manciple had the most time; Blow at least was in his own house, and it was his housekeeper who was stabbed; and Miss Fisk—what about Miss Fisk?"

"Miss Fisk is the only one who thought I was dead, sir."

"Yes. Elkins, we may make a detective of you yet—if you live long enough."

"We better find that knife."

"I don't think you are in any further danger from it. Still, it would be nice to have it in our hands. Our next job had better be to find out which of that precious bunch mucked up your nice jacket; and, incidentally, I'd like to know how it is a junior detective constable can afford a better suit than his superior officer."

"My sister Annie's intended, Wilf, works for the Nonpareil Clothing Company in Trafalgar Road, sir."

"Well, put your jacket on again; we'll go and visit."

The first call proved fruitless. Miss Fisk's door still displayed the notice: "Gone to tea with Dr. Blow next door if Urgent," and the only difference was that the empty milk bottle was gone and the notice was now propped against a full one.

"Either that means she hasn't been back, or she's very deep indeed," observed the Inspector.

"Don't forget she goes in and out up the wall, sir."

"I'll believe that when I see it."

At Dr. Blow's door they were more fortunate. Here, no notice gave news of his absence and, moreover, as they approached, the

Doctor's voice came strongly through the glass panels: "Don't knock! Don't ring! I can see you!"

It was Detective-Constable Elkins' first visit to the flat since the day he had been carried out ignominiously, feet first. He looked about him with interest; his daily duties seldom took him into the establishment of an elderly scholar. There they all were, the rows of leather-bound books, looking at once clever and dull. The prints, after Hogarth, of incidents in the life of Sir Hudibras, were neatly framed in black with gilt edges. The everlasting flowers looked somewhat self-conscious in an empty pickle jar from which Dr. Blow had not deemed it necessary to remove the label. There were the vintage typewriter; the card, dated 1937, propped against the desk calendar for 1934, the first announcing a lecture at the Royal Society of Literature and the second offering a perpetual reminder of the order of days in May of that distant year. All exactly as ever—except for the pickle jar. And Dr. Blow was the same, too, except that Elkins had never seen him before in a scarlet felt skull-cap with a tassel.

"Ah!" said the Doctor, the decoration bobbing over his eyes. "Just so! I saw you. Well, come in. What is it this time?"

When they were all seated in the Doctor's study—Blow himself in his big chair surrounded with its rampart of tables and piled up books; Urry, opposite, somewhat uncomfortable because his was the chair with the eccentric system of springs; and Elkins on a Windsor which creaked every time he breathed in—the Inspector began carefully. "A small point, sir. Hardly more than routine, but necessary to clear up for completeness. On the unfortunate occasion of the discovery of your housekeeper's body, you will recall that while I was taking a statement from Professor Manciple you went into the kitchen to eat some fried eggs. Detective Constable Elkins was lying on the floor, as you have told us. You ignored him and quietly ate your meal. That is so, is it not?"

"Perfectly accurate, except that I did not ignore the Constable completely. When I first went in and saw him, I distinctly remember a feeling of surprise. I said to myself something like, 'Oh, no, not again; well, this time it can wait.' I thought he was dead, you know. I would never delay calling for help while life remained, please don't think that. But cold fried eggs are really most unappetizing . . . yes. There seemed to be no hurry, you know; there he was, poor fellow. Er—I hope the attack has passed safely off?"

"Yes, sir. And what else did you do, besides eating your eggs?"

"Well, you know, I read a little. It aids digestion. There was only the meter card—ha ha! I remember rendering its salient points into idiomatic Greek—a pretty exercise, because, of course, there was nothing comparable with the South Eastern Gas Board in ancient Athens. I don't suppose there is today, come to that. Not a progressive corner of the world, you know."

"And what else did you do? *Did you wipe a large bloody knife on the back of the Constable's coat?*"

"Really, Inspector! Certainly not. I take it you mean a knife stained with blood. No, certainly. And the other knife, with egg on, I naturally left for Mrs. Sollihull, as one does. I had forgotten, you see, that there would be no washing up done. Miss Angell was a little appalled, I fear, when she came. My new housekeeper, you know. I call her Miss Angell; it's her name."

"And you didn't *see* a knife with blood on it, sir?"

"No. Er, Inspector, ought I not to have a witness . . . ?"

"Not unless you feel that the answers to my questions might be calculated to incriminate you. And then it is a matter for your solicitor. But, as I explained—I wonder, though, if it *is* merely a routine point. I must be honest with you. Perhaps you will feel you would like to call your solicitor?"

"Manciple will do. He has a very clear head. Let me telephone him. But I have said all I can on this point. I wiped no knife; I saw no knife. Is this the knife that poor Mrs. Sollihull—the woman, Elsie, you know; I call them Sollihull—was destroyed with?"

"The woman was stabbed, and according to your evidence and that of Professor Manciple, when her body was found the knife was sticking in her back. When we came, Dr. Blow, it was gone."

"Let me telephone Manciple."

The telephoning to Manciple took barely five minutes all told, and within a very short time the Professor was with them in the study, sitting poised on the edge of Dr. Blow's desk.

"To question you, sir, in the presence of a third party is not strictly regular; but I will do it because we are only going over old ground. Will you tell us again what passed in the kitchen when you were there frying eggs. Did the Detective-Constable complain of feeling unwell?"

"Not at all; and, indeed, it would not have been easy for him to do so. Most of the time he had his mouth full of buttered toast."

"Did he *look* unwell?"

"No."

"He was wearing his jacket, of course?"

"Of course."

"A man eating hot buttered toast—it was nice and crisp, I have no doubt—makes a loud crunching noise. It impairs even an acute hearing. You could have crept up behind him unnoticed and wiped a bloody knife on the back of his coat, couldn't you? Did you, in fact?"

"No. Let me explain, Inspector. First, I hadn't got a bloody knife. Next, he was sitting with his back to the wall on a chair between the gas stove and the sink. If I'd crawled along the wall behind the stove, I'd have got burnt; and if I'd crept over the sink, I'd have got wet. The whole proposition is foolish, quite foolish."

"I see you have a badly burned thumb."

"No doubt. And as you are so observant, you will have seen on that occasion that I had not a badly burned thumb. The injury is of later occurrence. Check—if that is the expression."

"Check," said the Inspector. "Then we must fall back on Miss Fisk."

"May we know what this inquiry portends?"

"Someone, sir—I'm not saying whom—wiped a large bloody knife on the back of the Constable's jacket while he was lying unconscious. And, as you may recall, we are looking for a large bloody knife."

"A knife with blood on, you know," Blow explained.

"I say," Manciple put in, "I say, look here. You keep calling him Detective-Constable. He was a Police-Constable, I distinctly remember: blue trousers, helmet, and all that. You couldn't wipe anything on the lining of his coat, done up with a belt and all that. Hey?"

Elkins slowly turned a brick red. "My promotion was retrospective to January, sir," he said desperately. "You know that. You recommended it."

"Come into the hall," Urry said. "Wait, gentlemen."

He led his subordinate out of the room, and then said savagely, "Why didn't you remind me? Now look what fools we seem! And what was it on your suit that you put in five shillings for the cleaning of, eh?"

"It was lipstick sir, after the police ball. My girl, Edith, couldn't come, and Constable Rice, Maude, what's in Superintendent Mullen's office . . ."

"Elkins, if it wasn't that the only alternative is Abner, I'd have you back on the beat tomorrow! And, anyhow, if it was lipstick I don't see how you got a gash in the back of your jacket six inches long. Not that it matters."

"I got it caught on Maudie's belt."

"You got it caught on Maudie's belt. And here am I practically accusing two respectable gentlemen of murder, all on account of Maudie's belt!"

"But, sir, the knife *was* missing, sir. You're entitled to ask them about it. Perhaps they washed it under the kitchen sink? Shall we ask them that?"

"Get back in there and try not to look the fool you are; and when we get back to the station you can tear up that chit for five shillings and think very carefully before you ask me to sign anything else.

"Now, gentlemen,"—and the Inspector returned to the attack —"now, gentlemen, that knife disappeared. Where did it go? Who took it? Why? Where is it now? These are the important questions!"

"That may be so, Inspector," Professor Manciple answered

firmly, "but I must tell you that in my opinion we employ police officers not merely to pose questions but to provide answers. Who took it? Where is it? Why? Dr. Blow and I eagerly await your solution."

"He is teasing you, Inspector," Blow put in. "See how pink he has gone."

Manciple gave a little high-pitched giggle and said, "I spy with my little eye," and waved a hand airily.

Detective-Constable Elkins stood up from his chair and said, "Cool"

Inspector Urry said nothing, but his mouth fell open and his eyes nearly started from his head. In the middle of Dr. Blow's desk lay *the* knife.

15

It was hardly in Miss Fisk's nature to look furtive, especially when she was wearing the dowager duchess' hat, which she had been assured was decorated (or had been) with bird-of-paradise plumage. But she could take as reasonable precautions as the next. That was why she now climbed the stairs to her flat in stocking feet. However, she might have spared herself the trouble, for Detective-Constable Elkins was standing at her front door, patiently waiting.

"Good morning, ma'am," he said politely.

"Good morning, Officer," Miss Fisk said, gracious in defeat. "Would you be waiting for me? I hope you have not waited long? I have been spending the night away—an old varsity friend, you know. We like to chat about old times once in a while."

"Inspector Urry's compliments, ma'am, and might he have an urgent word with you? He is in Dr. Blow's flat."

"I must just take in the milk, because it turns sour if left on the landing. And I want to change my shoes, you know. These are a little tight; but they were only sixteen and eleven, that was why I risked it, reduced from sixty-three. Wait, will you?"

Elkins didn't wait; he followed her in. She picked up two letters and thrust them into her bag, put the milk on the window sill under a large red earthenware cover, laced up her shoes—the same ones—and then said, "Now."

Elkins, anxious to redeem his damaged reputation, had been narrowly observing everything in sight in the hope of happening upon a clue, but, unluckily, for one not trained to pigeon-hole miscellaneous facts at breakneck speed, Miss Fisk's flat was noticeably overfurnished. Framed photographs, pottery animals, glass vases, brass candlesticks, tin boxes with the Stag at Eve on one side and a biscuit-maker's name on the other, books and magazines, and pieces of partly finished knitting—these were but the most obvious sundries in sight. The furniture itself was equally prodigal and miscellaneous: tables, chairs, chests of drawers, corner cupboards, Welsh dressers, coal boxes and work-boxes, and tin trunks and fiber trunks. The only thing Elkins saw that struck him as significant was on the shelf over the sink in the little cooking alcove which opened out of the larger room. Here were honey pots and jam pots and potted meat pots, and tins and jars and packets and bottles, and among them a tall cardboard cylinder with a green label boldly printed in yellow and white: "Ground Almonds." It was three-quarters full, the Detective discovered, squinting in at the top. Not full enough to have been bought in the last week or so—unless Miss Fisk put a pinch each morning in her early tea or soaked her corns in it—and too full to have justified her in seeking to borrow ground almonds elsewhere. The small discovery wasn't much, but it was something. The cylinder disappeared into Elkins' pocket, wrapped in a chance-found wisp of crochet work.

"Now!" said Miss Fisk, again.

She had not noticed, he thought. "Now, madam," said Elkins, formally and severely, as though the momentary delay were hers, and he escorted her to the Doctor's flat.

"Now, madam," Urry said, a few minutes later.

Dr. Blow looked keenly at Miss Fisk. She seemed the same as ever, and yet—as he knew—only a few hours since, she had been behaving in a manner quite scandalous in her years and state. Quite scandalous. And Manciple, came to that. . . . Really, underneath the most ordinary exteriors people maintained secret lives of rich complexity. The Doctor sighed, wondering if perhaps a life devoted exclusively to annotating the English classics had not here and there excluded him from engaging mysteries.

"Now, madam," Urry was saying, "please tell us if you have ever seen this before." He held out to her, blade first, the famous knife.

It had a broad blade about six inches long, tapering to a point. It was obviously heavy, and the handle was bound about with brass. It shone dully. The Inspector held it by the haft, between finger and thumb, leaving the main handle free. As she put out her hand to take it, he said sharply, "Don't touch it!"

"I believe my brother had one like that when he was a Scout-master," Miss Fisk said, "but he emigrated to Canada, you know. It wouldn't be his, because he took everything with him, except the tinted photograph of my grandmother. What a very dangerous article, Inspector, when you see it close up. I am surprised they let little boys have them."

"This is a very dangerous article indeed, as you say, Miss Fisk."

"It's the one Mrs. Sollihull had in her back," Manciple explained.

Inspector Urry turned on him like a flash. "Oh, is it, sir!" he said. "Is it? Well, you have the advantage of having had an opportunity of inspecting it *in situ,* so to say. We have been less fortunate. So you identify the weapon?"

"I'm going by you," Manciple said mildly. "You said 'That's it!' when you saw it. You can hardly be looking for two knives, now can you?"

"Surely it's the one that was in Millie's butter?" Dr. Blow asked, peering closely at the knife, which still lay lightly in the Inspector's hand. "You remember, Manciple?"

"Yes, yes,"—impatiently—"don't fidget, Blow. The Inspector has heard all about that; we told him."

"Did you say Millie?" said Miss Fisk, faintly. "Give me a little air!" She groped her way to the window, holding her hand to her face and muttering, "Air! Air!"

"Mind!" cried Manciple, "she'll crawl off somewhere, like as not. Only open it an inch!"

"Don't open it at all," said Inspector Urry. "The room is full of perfectly good air already. Miss Fisk, you must please pull yourself together. Take a deep breath. There's air enough for everybody. And then, tell us, please, why do you put your hand before your face and ask for air when Dr. Blow says 'Millie.'

Tell us that!"

"You are ruthless, ruthless," Miss Fisk said. "Well, if I do tell you, you leave me alone after that. I'm not young, Inspector, I admit it. And I am not in robust health. It has all been a great shock, and now this on top of it. Millie spreading butter with a murderer's knife!"

"Begin at the beginning," Manciple suggested. "It wasn't ground almonds you came to borrow, was it?"

Elkins, with an air of quiet triumph, produced his little surprise. "Ground almonds, sir," he said. "About half a pound of the stuff. In Miss Fisk's flat."

"That's my curry powder," Miss Fisk said. "Give it to me at once; I shall need it for last Friday's bit of mutton."

"It says ground almonds," began Elkins, dubiously. He sniffed at the powder.

"Curry," said the Inspector. "I can smell that much from here. Give the lady her curry, Elkins. Madam, my Detective-Constable is very conscientious, but they never give them curry —or ground almonds, come to that—in the police barracks. He never knew."

"Well, I hope he hasn't got my bit of Friday's mutton in his other pocket," said Miss Fisk. "It needs a pinch of curry by Tuesday, you know."

"Now, madam," Urry prompted. "What will you wish to tell us? Elkins will take your statement. I must ask Dr. Blow and Professor Manciple to excuse us. This, of course, is confidential. Perhaps we ought to go to the police station; after all, this is the Doctor's study. Or we could go to Miss Fisk's place."

"I'd rather they heard it all. I am not ashamed. And Dr. Blow has a right to know, indeed a perfect right. He has had a fortunate escape, Dr. Blow has. When I think of that woman."

"Which woman?"

"Mrs. Sollihull, as he calls her. Elsie. We were at school together at Alma Road. Gone, now, bombed. But this was years ago. Well, then I was secretary-companion to the dowager duchess, and Elsie went to London. I never saw her for years, and I was keeping company with a young man called George James Gilstrap, who was a superior, very gentlemanly fellow, though in a coal merchants. It was all understood between us, and then one day Elsie turned up with her London ways and a manner of walking which I can only call wanton, and poor George, who was weak although superior, was led away. They used to go bicycling together, until one day he came to me ever so ashamed and said she had gone off with his watch."

"Yes?"

"Well, you see, she had gone off with his watch, which was a very good one that had belonged to his father, and George's head was turned and he only had me to come to. He wanted her back. Of course, I said don't be a fool, James—I used to call him James when I was angry—you let her steal your father's watch and then you want her back. Some people, I said to him, know how to be true and loyal and behave right, and other people don't know when they are well off. I didn't like to speak too plainly, because we were on the top of a tram. She never came back, and me and George used to see something of one another, but it was never the same; and then, of course, there was the war and we lost touch. You know how you get shifted about. And I lost his address and I never saw him again."

"This is a painful story, madam. I'm sorry you have to tell us all your personal affairs in this way. Especially as, so far, I must confess I can't see how it helps my inquiry, except to show that Flash Elsie was up to her tricks from an early age, and heaven knows we already knew that. Twenty convictions and over sixty other cases taken into account, and goodness knows how many others—like your George's watch—that were never pinned on her."

"It had a gold chain," Miss Fisk observed. "As for your inquiry, I'm coming to that. One day, when I was revolving the sad vicissitudes of my life and thinking if I'd had my time over again I'd have gone to Canada with my brother and made a clean break, I remembered that George used to keep his address on a slip of paper pasted in the back of his watch, in case he was ever knocked off his bike. Although it was a very nice watch it wasn't of great value, and although it was a man's watch it wasn't very big. I reckoned Elsie might keep it, because she could never get a watch to go on her wrist, and this was one she could carry in her bag. So I decided to track her down and get it back for George. If that didn't soften him, with everything that had been between us, too, and it being his father's watch as well, I thought nothing would. But I felt sure it would soften George, who was not a bad sort, and now he had left the coal merchants he might have bettered himself, come to that. It was worth trying."

"She wouldn't have kept his address stuck in the back," Professor Manciple said.

"You don't know Elsie," said Miss Fisk. "She never wasted anything. She'd have kept it, all right, in case she ever wanted to go back and steal his cufflinks, which were very superior for a young man in his station: silver and enamel, with the monogram F.S."

"That wasn't George's monogram," said Inspector Urry.

"You couldn't see it unless you looked close," Miss Fisk explained. "They had been the duke's; the dowager duchess sold them to me. She had no use for them, but she hated giving things away. She never gave me anything except for what was in her will, but sometimes she used to say, 'Ellen, that hat would suit your style very well; I'm sick of seeing it about, although it's the one the Queen commented on. Give me fifteen shillings and it's yours.' So I used to save up and pay her and have the hat. I gave George the links for Christmas, and he never even noticed the monogram. I'm only telling you because Elsie knew silver; I'll say that for her. But she had some sense of shame. She'd never have taken them while they were out bicycling and let him go home with a draft running up his arms."

"Well. So what did you do?"

"I used to spend my holidays looking for her, and after the dowager duchess died and left me what she did—it wasn't much, but I manage—I spent a great deal of time following Elsie. Sometimes it wasn't her after all. I didn't dare advertize, you see, so I used to ask the minister if any of the congregation had a house-keeper called Elsie. But Elsie never kept a job long; I don't know why. Very often, I was too late and she'd gone. She'd gone at West Moors when I got there, and at Fowey, and at Barnet. And at Arundel, too. Finally, I met her on the stairs, here, when I wasn't even thinking of her. So I pulled my hat over my eyes and stood in the shadow and blurted out anything I could think of in a disguised voice and passed it off. Then I came in that evening, not expecting anything, you know, and I got the shock of my life when the lights were on and policemen everywhere. Then I saw the one that I thought was dead, and I screamed. And that's how it was."

"So you lied to me when you said you had come to borrow ground almonds."

"Well, no. I *was* out of ground almonds; and if she'd been awake and said anything I'd have asked for some. Always handy, they are. But, of course, what I hoped to do was find it ticking on the table by her bed or hanging on the dresser in the kitchen."

"Did you go into the housekeeper's room, Miss Fisk?"

"Oh, no!—I wouldn't dream—besides, it was locked."

"That didn't stop you the next night," Manciple pointed out. "But, I forgot. That night you were wearing an extra wooly."

"Well, you see, as it wasn't a wrist watch I knew it wouldn't be on the body," Miss Fisk explained. "It wouldn't be in her handbag, either, even if they took that with them when they took her away—and I couldn't see why they should, not on a stretcher, not to the mortuary, not like if it was to hospital and she was only ill-like."

"Not in her handbag, no." Dr. Blow murmured.

"Oh, sir? And how are you aware of that?"

"Because I looked. Not for her watch, for her cards, you know. I give them the money, you know, and they stamp them themselves. But I am not a hard man, and it struck me that she might have forgotten to do it; some do it once a month, you know, although it says do it every week. Well, what if she hadn't done it, and now this? You get buried for nothing, you know, so they tell me, if you produce the card properly stamped. So I went to find it, but it wasn't there. I didn't see any watch, either, and I was keeping an eye open because Manciple said her watch wasn't there."

"Why was Professor Manciple interested in Mrs. Sollihull's watch?"

"Because . . ."

"I'm here," Manciple interrupted. "I can answer for myself. I was not in the least interested in the woman's watch. I have one of my own. I merely said her watch wasn't under her pillow, and we knew that well enough because before making three slices of burnt toast Miss Fisk had stripped the bed."

"Stripped the bed?"

"Stripped it and ripped it. If Miss Angell is not in it just now, you might care to inspect the scar."

"She sewed it very neatly; I saw it," Dr. Blow said. "And she put the feathers back, too. Yes, let us go and look. Miss Angell has gone to visit her late first husband's mother this afternoon. I always know, because there is a smell of cheese cakes in the morning. Miss Angell's late first husband's mother likes them. Of course, she buys her own cheese, and I say nothing about the gas. The woman is giving complete satisfaction."

"I wouldn't have one who'd buried two husbands," Professor Manciple remarked, "but Blow is very confiding."

"She keeps up with both their mothers, Manciple. That's a good sign. She'd have to be a hypocrite. And, besides, all house-keepers are not murderers or victims of murder. I foresee a useful life here for Miss Angell for many years. I'll just tap on the door, you know. You are all here as witnesses. Just so—she is out. Come in; it is a very sunny room, and neat. Very neat. Perhaps Miss Fisk would be kind enough to lift out the night clothes, if there are any; and then we can turn back the under sheet . . . ah! Thank you, exactly so."

Miss Fisk had briskly performed the office assigned to her and now stood with a blue-dotted nightgown draped over her arm. Dr. Blow turned back the bedclothes, rolling them up as he went, and at last as they gathered round he said in triumph, "There!"

Across the striped stuff of the mattress there was a long, neat scar where it had been sewn up. It was a beautiful piece of needle-work, and nearly invisible, unless one were looking for it.

"Very nice," said the Inspector. "Well . . ."

As they all leaned over Elkins accidently jostled Dr. Blow and threw him forward onto the mattress, knocking him breathless for a moment. The others jumped back, and Urry hastened to give him a hand up. But Dr. Blow, panting, said between gasping breaths, "It is nothing, nothing. Pray leave me. I can hear something ticking."

He placed his good ear close to the mattress, and held up a hand, motioning for silence.

"What can it be?" asked Miss Fisk. "It can hardly be a bomb, I hope."

"A bed tick," murmured Manciple, going a little pink.

"Just here," Blow said. "Manciple, my dear fellow, lend me your pocket nail scissors. Thank you, yes."

Delicately, he inserted the little pointed blade into the mattress and began to make an incision. A few feathers oozed out, and then, "Here!" cried the Doctor, and he drew out a small gold watch.

"I said it was on a chain," Miss Fisk said, and there the chain was without a doubt. They could all hear the watch ticking.

"Give it to me!" said the Inspector. In his customary careful manner he handled it without spoiling any surface that might carry fingerprints, and, luckily, Blow had pulled it out by the chain.

"Lend me the scissors, sir." The Inspector took them, and slid the point under the flap at the back. With a little click, the hinge turned and the lid came up. A tiny piece of paper cut into a circle was wedged inside.

The Inspector lifted it and read the faint, faded writing on it: "George James Gilstrap, 18 Stanmer Road, Seven Dials, Winton."

"That was it!" said Miss Fisk. "You went up two steps to the front door. Fancy me forgetting!"

"It's been crossed out," Inspector Urry said, "so you needn't make a note of it. He obviously left. There's another address on the other side. Ah, and a most interesting one at that. Can anyone guess what it is?"

"I'm not sure he didn't move to Taunton, . . ." Miss Fisk began, but the Professor interrupted.

"Would it be eight hundred and fourteen B Mile End Road," he said softly.

"It not only would, but it is," said Inspector Urry.

16

"If that chap Gilstrap's changed his name I give up; there are far too many people in this case with different names," Inspector Urry said. "Flash Elsie's all right, because, after all, you can't expect the criminal classes to advertize themselves. Carter or Cuttle, it's all one; it's still Flash Elsie. But if it turns out she was Mrs. Gilstrap after all, I pass. It would mean she hadn't even stolen the watch, not so as we could have acted, I mean. She'd say she borrowed it."

"She'd say that anyway," Miss Fisk observed. "She was plausible, was Elsie, that I give her. Very smooth."

"Look here," Manciple said, "people may put their watch under the pillow, even if it is a stolen one. But they don't sew it up every night inside the mattress. Life's too short. Now, then."

"Just what I was coming to," the Inspector agreed. "Suppose the person who ripped up the mattress wasn't taking it out, but *putting it in?*"

"I won't have anything to do with it," Miss Fisk said. "I simply came in to borrow a penn'orth of gas and make a slice of toast. George Gilstrap can go hang, and his watch with him, for all I care."

"Were you making toast the nights the mattresses were ripped at Barnet, Bournemouth, Fowey, and Arundel?" the Professor asked.

"Very good, Gideon," Dr. Blow said. "And don't forget West Moors."

"I may have changed my mind," Miss Fisk answered darkly.

The Inspector changed the subject. "Dr. Blow," he said, "there is another little thing we might as well clear up, since we are all being very frank with one another. How did you know that piece of paper was tucked into Mrs. Sollihull's stocking?"

"Oh, it is simple, Inspector. Everyone knows they either tuck it in their stocking or in their shoe—under the instep, you know, Manciple, but only if it isn't bulky, and not, of course, if they have fallen arches. Where was I? Yes, or down the front of their dress. Well, that's where Mrs. Sollihull kept her pocket handkerchief. So it must have been in her stocking, just tucked in at the top, you know. Merely an assumption on my part; I had no positive knowledge, I assure you."

"Or in her shoe?"

"Sometimes corpses have things clutched in the hand, you know—hair, bits of cloth, mud, and so on. Clues, you know, Gideon, as I have told you of."

"Yes, William. But you have not answered the Inspector's question, you know."

"I'll ask *you* a question, Inspector. How did you know I knew it was tucked in the top of her stocking?"

"The Professor told me."

"Blow, my dear fellow . . ."

"Be silent, Gideon. I perfectly understand your motives. You were unwilling for the Inspector to know the fragment of writing was yours. I can sympathize; it is not a thing I should care to admit myself. One really hasn't time for frivolous pursuits of that sort; but, of course, a man who can waste his evenings sitting in a picture palace has a lower standard of critical morality and integrity, I suppose."

"Don't be absurd, Blow. I merely needed the money. A house full of coins that nobody will accept doesn't insure things to eat, you know."

"You needed money, my dear fellow!" The Doctor put his hand in his pocket and brought out a handful of silver, three crumpled notes, a handkerchief, a piece of red sealing wax, and half an apple.

"What exactly is this?" The Inspector demanded.

130

Miss Fisk was all attention, too. She always needed money, even half a crown and the lump of red sealing wax (to which it was adhering) would have served.

Manciple threw up his hands in a despairing gesture and said, "The most natural thing in the world, Inspector. But one is a little shy, naturally. *The Hibbert Journal,* you know; a guinea for the best version in Greek of Wordsworth's Westminster Bridge sonnet. I had roughed something out one evening when they were serving peanuts and ices, you know, and the lights were on. Then I noticed that inadvertently I had headed it 'from the Greek' and of course it was not 'from,' not at all, but quite the reverse. So I tore the top off."

"And what did you do with it?"

"Oh, well, I suppose I must have dropped it in Blow's flat or something. But it was definitely in the Odeon I tore it off."

"In the *Odeon!* And I suppose the film was *Rock 'n' Roll Blues?*"

"Check," said Professor Manciple.

"Check," said Inspector Urry.

Blow beamed. "Manciple, my dear fellow, I misjudged you! Pray allow me to apologize. I thought you had been in some way indiscreet!"

"Very natural, Blow, very natural. Say nothing more about it, I beg. But all the same, I'd like very much to know how my piece of paper came to be tucked into her stocking."

"What I want to know," said Detective-Constable Elkins, "is did you win the guinea?"

"I forgot to send it up," Manciple confessed, "but judging by the version that did—by Einstein of Worms, Blow—I ought to have done."

"I didn't think you could prove it," said Detective-Constable Elkins. He wrote something in his book.

"And now, Miss Fisk," the Inspector said, again changing the subject, "will you please tell me why you cried 'Air! Air!' when Dr. Blow said 'Millie'?"

"It was a palpitation, Inspector. I am subject to them, when in a warm room."

"No doubt, madam, and I'm sorry for it. But why did 'Millie' bring it on?"

"I don't know what you mean."

"I said 'Millie's butter,' you know," the Doctor said kindly, "and you said 'Give me air.'"

"I have entirely forgotten the incident."

"But it's hardly ten minutes ago."

"Inspector, I must ask you not to cross-question me about my health, which is a confidential matter between myself and my doctor. I was a little unwell, that is all. As for Millie, which is an absurd name unless for a canary, I know no such person. And now, if you will excuse me, I will go home."

The Inspector shrugged his shoulders. "Very well, madam. I will not detain you. . . ."

"I should hope not, indeed!"

"Elkins, accompany the lady home."

Urry had no intention of going home just yet. He settled himself back, sinking deeper in the sofa, and crossed his legs. He looked at Blow with speculation in his eyes, and the Doctor looked back with a puzzled expression. He could have sworn that when Miss Fisk went they had all gone—except Manciple, of course. Yet, here was the Inspector! Perhaps he was waiting to be asked to take a cup of tea, that must be it. A senior police official could not be dismissed in the way one sent away a constable. Exactly so.

However, the Inspector wasn't thirsty for tea, but for information. He politely declined refreshment, and pressed on with his inquiries.

"You say, gentlemen, that you visited the Greek Street Agency and found an electric furnace in the cellar, and you, Professor Manciple, found a quantity of silverplate concealed in the offices."

"And gold."

"And gold. Most interesting, gentlemen. You were more successful than Detective-Constable Elkins, who couldn't even find the address. It turned out he had spent the morning prosecuting his inquiries in Beak Street—I'm not saying this in order to tell tales, you must understand, but so that you will see that my work is not made easier merely because I have several men under my orders. A policeman's lot is not a happy one."

"Gilbert, you know, Manciple," Dr. Blow explained. He began to hum a little tune.

"I know; I know," his friend answered, a little testily. "They made it into a film." He began to hum also.

"Gentlemen," the Inspector went on, "I must visit this secret store of yours. I'd also like to see the place in Carlisle Street, but I'm much afraid I'd never get an expenses chit passed for three pounds. And that, incidentally, brings us back to Millie. Miss Fisk was undoubtedly most disturbed at the name. Why?"

"We never actually saw Millie, you know," the Doctor reminded him.

"Nor Florrie, come to that. But I suppose a daily woman wouldn't be much help."

"Anything helps, when you're beginning at the beginning," Urry said feelingly. "Do you realize that we know little more now than we knew on the morning Flash Elsie was found dead? We know a lot of mixed up, unrelated facts, many of them irrelevant. But we have no idea who stabbed your housekeeper, Dr. Blow, nor why. In the morning I shall go up to London myself and look around."

"There's my silver vase, too. Don't forget that."

"I have your silver vase very much in mind, sir. But the other affair is murder—murder, gentlemen. That's something else we must never forget. Now, Professor Manciple. You say you composed your poem in the cinema—it was the Odeon, I think— during the interval between films. And you threw away the piece of paper that was spoiled. Did you see who was sitting near you, in front and at the sides; I suppose you didn't toss the fragment back over your shoulder? You'd hardly do that."

"I didn't *compose* the poem, you know. I made a rough version in Greek, from memory of the original. And I jotted down the salient points on the bit of paper, and just tore off the top when I saw I had foolishly written 'from the Greek.' I remember now. I pushed it down beside the seat; I didn't throw it anywhere."

"Beside the seat—do you mean into the space between your seat and the next?"

"Well, yes, I suppose so. I wasn't looking. I felt a sort of strap, come to think of it, and I just pushed the piece of paper in. I only wanted to be rid of it; I wasn't thinking about it much, you know."

"And you didn't see any of your near neighbors?"

"No. What with the price of seats today, if I go to the cinema I keep my eyes on the screen. Even then I doubt if you get your value. Half the time they seem to be busy telling you to buy ices."

"I'll tell you what I think, sir. I think that sort of strap you thought you felt was Mrs. Sollihull's garter."

"Really, Inspector!"

"Please don't be offended. Such a mishap might befall anybody, especially if he never took his eyes off the screen. And in a dark place like a cinema, you might easily not notice that Dr. Blow's housekeeper was sitting beside you."

"Then if she was at the cinema," Blow began eagerly, "it must have been her day off—Wednesday, you know—just as I thought!"

"It was Tuesday, sir, Tuesday. But if Mrs. Sollihull went to the pictures on a Tuesday, she might not wish to be seen by Professor Manciple, you understand. Playing truant, she was, eh?"

"It would certainly explain why I never had my tea. I don't care to criticize a woman who has left my service, Inspector, but now I come to think of it, I called her several times during that fortnight and she never came. I call them, you know, and then if they don't come I forget that I have called them. But it is very wrong actually to go off like that to a cinema and not leave me my tea. I hope they don't all do that. Where is Miss Angell, I wonder?"

"Blow, my dear fellow, you yourself told us she was taking cheese cakes to her late first husband's mother; and it isn't tea time yet. Have you looked in the kitchen to see if she left you a tray?"

"I remember now. Just so. It is her day for cheese cakes, of course. There was a smell of them this morning."

"There's no smell of them now. I suppose she took the lot. I could just fancy a cheese cake."

"It was her cheese, you know."

Inspector Urry wondered if very learned men always engaged in this sort of cross talk when they found themselves together. Personally, he preferred football as a topic. He stood up. "Well, gentlemen," he said, "I'll be off. Tomorrow I shall go along to Greek Street and see what I can pick up. We must make a little progress soon; we can't always be out of luck. Good day!"

The Chief Constable said, "Well, Urry. Is that you?"

The Inspector set down the knife and the watch and proceeded to tell his story, ending up sadly with, "No recognizable fingerprints, sir, only Elkins' thumb on the blade. Nothing on the watch worth having, but I'll obviously have to go up and look into the London angle myself. Miss Fisk is the deep one, I reckon; an answer to everything, she has."

"That's more than you have, Urry."

"I'll get the answers, never fear, sir. But I think I shall have to put in a chit for three pounds. Now, these are the points we are clear on: first, 'The Greek.' He's a knife short; he was hanging about that night, I'm convinced of it. And his real name's Cuttle, I swear. Next, Miss Ellen Fisk. She knows more than she admits; I've let Elkins loose on her; he's Chapel. Take her to a whist drive, as like as not. Then the London end. Alf and this boy they talk about. And the place in Mile End Road, and all that stolen silver and the electric furnace in the basement. I blame the Metropolitan boys, you know; but I suppose they're kept pretty busy with parking offences, just as we are. I've not seen hide nor hair of Temple since Tuesday."

"You're not likely to; I've given him to Inspector Burge, and Wix. Sorry, Urry, but Burge is rushed off his feet, what with barrow boys and cycles without rear lights and young couples on the golf links and that."

"Well, sir, I suppose it means fewer people to share the credit when we do run him down. Where was I? Ah! Yes. Miss Fisk. I'm dealing with her. Then there's that Miss Emily Cakebread, not sleeping in her bed and generally getting about suspiciously. I've time for a word with her now, I fancy. Will you excuse me if I get off?"

"You won't have much competition," said the Chief Constable with a laugh.

That was rather good. He began reconstructing the scene in his mind for later discussion with his wife. Urry said . . . I said. . . .

"Cut along, Urry," said the Chief Constable.

The Inspector departed.

When Inspector Urry reached Cakebread's Domestic Agency it was well after five o'clock. He half-expected to find the office closed, but it was not. Miss Cakebread was just tidying up before going home. Of Miss Emily Cakebread there was no sign.

"Yes?" said Miss Cakebread sharply. For a moment she mistook the Inspector for a domestic. Then she recognized him and she said more temperately, "Oh, it is the police sergeant."

"Good evening, madam," began Inspector Urry, taking off his hat. "I am sorry to trouble you, but as I promised, I am now following up the intelligence you gave me that Miss Emily Cakebread had not slept in her bed on two nights recently when, for other reasons, I am interested in accounting for the whereabouts of certain persons. Is Miss Emily available for me to speak to?"

"No, she is not. She had been absent from the office all day, and I have been greatly inconvenienced. I have no other assistant to work the telephone and the typewriter, and I have been forced to write to a most valued client in longhand, besides twice having to interrupt interviews with clients of title in order to answer the telephone."

"When you say she is absent, do you mean she is missing?"

"I mean I have no idea of her whereabouts. She was always a feckless child, and she may have done something foolish."

"We are speaking about the same person, I hope? Miss Emily Cakebread is the one I mean. Tall lady, gray, wears spectacles, about fifty?"

"My sister Emily is forty-seven, a comparatively young woman. Yes, of course it is she of whom I am speaking. If I called her a child it was merely a figure of speech. You must not be so precise."

"Madam, police work is essentially a matter of precision. Now, may I see the bed?"

"If you will wait one moment while I lock the office you may come home with me. There may be a message by now. Let me see—the lights are off. Yes, I have bolted the windows and doors. The gas fire is out. I have locked the strong box. The tap is not dripping—they freeze, you know, not in this weather, but a precaution neglected is a precaution wasted, my mother always used to say. She left off her flannel in April and caught a fatal chill. Well, come along then."

The Inspector walked somewhat self-consciously to the bus stop with Miss Cakebread. She was taller than he, and he felt her lack of confidence in his ability. However, she made no objection when he paid for her on the bus, and that was something; he'd had an uneasy feeling she meant to produce sixpence and ask for one and a half.

Miss Cakebread lived with her sister in a gloomy, late-Victorian villa of yellow brick, with bushes growing close up to the windows and a carriage drive all of twenty yards long. It looked damp and inhospitable, and when Miss Cakebread put her key in the door and opened it, a dank odor of boiled cabbage came wearily out to meet them.

"Effie!" Miss Cakebread called, and a thin maid came hurrying from the back parts of the house. "Take the gentleman's coat," said Miss Cakebread. "Officer, you will have some tea. Come into the drawing room. That miniature was a gift from Her Serene Highness. This is Her Serene Highness in the silver frame. We kept her in between maids for years."

The drawing room was full of mahogany furniture and leather chairs and ferns in pots. The pictures were all dull engravings after admired Victorian masters. The only object Inspector Urry really took a fancy to was a delicately fluted silver flower vase in which were half-a-dozen paper carnations and a sprig of everlasting fern. As Miss Cakebread fussed among the tea things the Inspector lifted the vase idly and glanced underneath at the heavy serge cloth covering the mantelpiece. The weight of the metal had barely marked the cloth, and yet a light photo frame on the other side of the mantel left a clear dent in the place from which it was lifted.

"I always take a cup of tea on returning home," Miss Cakebread said.

The Inspector accepted a cup and drank it. He stood up.

"You will forgive me, madam; I have much to do. May I just peep into Miss Emily Cakebread's room? You have received no message on your return home? There is no letter?"

"Nothing. I can see it all clearly enough. She has been made away with for her money."

"Has she money?"

"Certainly not, but naturally an assassin would hardly believe that. All she has is a workbox in mother-of-pearl that was given to her by Lady Sweetwater many years ago for assisting at a fête when we could not get trained domestics for love or money. The war, you know. I knew of a second footman who went into the Navy and came out an Admiral of the Fleet. He had the impertinence to send to us for a cook. Well, this is Emily's room."

Emily's room was small and dark, with dull green wallpaper and a brown varnished suite consisting of wardrobe, chest of drawers, dressing table, and washstand. The linoleum was green, the single rug brown. And the bed creaked.

It creaked dismally, and Emily sat up in it and screamed.

17

"Manciple," said Dr. Blow when they met next morning, "do you think we ought to go disguised? We must be pretty well known in Greek Street by now."

"False beards and tinted glasses are foolish, Blow. Whom could you get yourself up to look like but some other old man? If anybody says anything, make out you dropped something last time and you're looking for it. After all, the place isn't private. Anyone can pass that way. I can be helping you. But it won't arise, my dear fellow. The people in Greek Street are all too busy about their own affairs to take any notice of us."

The two old gentlemen had now abandoned any pretense at working. In Manciple's study a partly written paper on the Coinage of King Canute lay gathering dust, forgotten; although it had to be read before a learned society, several of whose members were already all agog, two weeks from that day. As for the whole works of Samuel Butler, the Doctor had so far put them behind him that he hadn't so much as murmured half a line from *Hudibras* for three days.

They were standing in Blow's hall, their hats on, ready to catch the early train, when suddenly the Doctor darted forward.

"Don't ring!" he cried. "Don't knock! I can see you!" and he opened the door to admit Miss Emily Cakebread.

"Good morning, Miss Emily. You are early. 'Up rose the sun,' just so. We must never despise Chaucer. If it's about the account, you know, I must ask you please to write, because I stick them on my file and I have no record if they're verbal."

"It is not about the account, Dr. Blow. I type them, but it is my sister who solicits payment and afterward demands it if they get overdue. Indeed, it is not you upon whom I have called, but upon Professor Manciple, if you will excuse my disturbing you. I felt assured he was here when I found he was out."

"You have been found out, Manciple! Ha! Well, if it is not about the account I think I'll just make a cup of cocoa while you are engaged together. They never seem to serve cocoa in trains now."

He wandered away to the kitchen, and might have been heard explaining to Miss Angell that cocoa—*theobroma cacao*—was a favorite drink with the Aztec Emperor Montezuma; but Manciple had led his visitor into the study and shut the door.

"Gideon!" she said at once, scarcely pausing before flinging herself into his arms. "My sister has put me out of the house. She disowns me! I am out of work. She won't even give me a reference. And she's sent my things down to the Wilberforce Temperance Guest House in a tin trunk."

Professor Manciple gently but firmly disentangled himself and led the lady to a chair. The sofa was softer, but he thought better of that, and put her on the Windsor chair that creaked. He remained standing, with Blow's desk between them. He had hoped and expected the incident in Greek Street to be at once isolated and unique, a strange memory, nothing more. And here she was calling him Gideon and breathing on him.

He assumed a brisk professional air, modeled on that of Inspector Urry following up a strong clue, and said, "Now, madam. You are distraught. Please collect yourself. And tell me what has happened."

"It was last night," Miss Emily Cakebread began tearfully. "After I got home the night before—you know, *that* night, Gideon dear—it was too late for me to retire"—here she blushed and lowered her eyes—"so I just loosened my corsets and read *Bleak House*. I was tired all next day and working under a great strain. I didn't know my sister had told the police, not then."

"Told the police! About what, pray?"

"About me not sleeping in my room that night. So in the

evening, as soon as I got home, I went to bed—I was tired—I always get home first because my sister does the lights and locks up. When my sister came home she brought that Police Inspector with her, and they came up to my room and I was in bed and it was awful."

"Awful?"

"A policeman in my room, and my sister saying 'Emily! Stay in bed at once!'—because I began getting up, you know. I thought it was the house on fire, them coming in like that. And when he was gone, she said I was wanton, going to bed like that at five o'clock, and where was I last night. So I said, 'I'm more than twenty-one'; and she said, 'More than forty-one!' "

"Pickwick," put in Professor Manciple, but the lady hurried on with her explanation.

"Then she said, 'Not in my dear mother's house, you don't!' and got out this tin trunk and began packing my things. So I came here as soon as I could, after passing the night at the Wilberforce Temperance Guest House."

"Is the Wilberforce not comfortable?"

"Very comfortable, and reasonable, too. But, Gideon, *I want a home!*"

"I'm much afraid Dr. Blow and I will miss our train," Professor Manciple said formally.

At this interesting juncture Dr. Blow entered. "Manciple," he said heartily, "ah, there you are. It is time we were going. I have been sitting in the kitchen, I can't think why. Oh, Miss Emily Cakebread! Good morning. If it's about the account . . ."

"It is not about the account, Dr. Blow. I have been conversing on a private matter with Professor Manciple, that is all."

"That must be why I was sitting in the kitchen, then," Dr. Blow responded with some relief. He liked all his actions to be ordered and rational.

"We must certainly leave now," Manciple said with decision. "Thank you, Miss Emily. I will give consideration to your case."

"Thank you, Professor," Miss Emily Cakebread answered faintly. She wished someone had offered her a cup of cocoa.

As the two old gentlemen proceeded up Greek Street Dr. Blow was still anxious not to be recognized, from some obscure conviction that the detective needs to be as anonymous as the criminal. No doubt he was right, but the theory was put to no severe test, for Greek Street happened to be almost deserted. It contributes rather less to the daytime activity of Soho than its immediate neighbors, because it contains fewer coffee bars and other points of rendezvous than they, and, indeed, it has one very long stretch of plain blank wall where the former Prince Edward Theatre rises like a cliff. Manciple had made no concessions to Blow's misgivings, and in view of this the Doctor's own half-hearted turning up of his coat collar and hunching of his shoulders was of theatrical rather than of practical effect. He merely looked as if he were suffering with a piece of grit in his shoe.

As they drew near to number three hundred Manciple said tensely, "Blow, there's a policeman there. Better walk straight past!"

"I should expect it is better to turn back," Blow observed, allowing his stride to slacken.

"No, come on, man. He's looking at us. If we turn now it will be highly suspicious."

"Possibly," Blow said, "but I wish you would tell me, my dear fellow, of what we can be accused merely for altering the direction of our progress along a public street. Hem—this is not an inquiry prompted by any impulse to sarcasm."

"I dare say not," Manciple answered drily. "For once, however, your powers of literary expression have not correctly interpreted the mind that directs them. The sarcasm is present, even though not intended. My answer, Blow, is unashamedly satirical. I take it a sense of rectitude is of greater value to you than personal liberty, etc. We have aroused a good deal of police suspicion. Let us not encourage more by idle folly. Just walk past naturally and the fellow may not even twig who we are. Scuttle about like a disturbed crab and we'll have the Flying Squad out after us before you can say 'Sir Eustace Grey.' "

"Well, in my view a false beard would have made all the difference," Blow replied, walking on.

As they drew level with the house, chatting quietly about the Martin Marprelate controversies of 1588–1589 so as to direct attention away from themselves, the constable at the door of number three hundred said, "Dr. Blow, sir."

"You don't know me," the Doctor said, peering closely at the man. "But I suppose you noticed the resemblance. I confess that I am Dr. Blow, if it is Dr. *William* Blow of whom you were thinking. There may well be others."

"Dr. Blow, sir, and Professor Manciple. I was warned to expect you, gentlemen. The Inspector would be obliged if you would step up."

As they mounted the stairs Manciple said, "Now look what fools we should have looked if we had come disguised."

"Oh, I don't know," the Doctor protested, "a false mustache can very readily be slipped into the pocket. It was never my intention, you know, to wear anything elaborate like a skirt. And if we had been wearing mustaches—this was my original assertion—we might not have been recognized. We could have walked past, or gone back, or even played with the policeman by asking him the time or the way to the Soane Museum."

"Huh! If I were a policeman and someone in a false mustache asked me the time I'd ring up the Soane Museum and tell them to lock up their Hogarths. And I'd ring up the National Gallery for good measure and get them to put the Rokeby Venus out of sight!"

"I sometimes wonder why they don't do that anyway. . . . Ah, Inspector!"

"Good morning, gentlemen. I was expecting you. You only just caught the train, though! Well, sit down, won't you?"

Inspector Urry was sitting at Alf's desk, very much at home. Of the staff there was no sign. Detective-Constable Elkins was in the outer office moodily turning over a pile of correspondence folders and occasionally saying "ah" bleakly under his breath. Professor Manciple's celebrated secret door stood wide open, but the cupboard within was empty. Urry was employed in the same way as Elkins, but with much the same apparent lack of result. Alf's desk, which ought to have contained the most interesting and intimate records of the domestic employment agency—if such things can ever be of wide general interest—had yielded only routine papers, most of them apparently bona-fide records of blameless transactions involving butlers, chauffeurs, and second parlor-maids. It had also yielded several bottles and boxes containing aspirin and other remedies in bewildering variety, and the expected complement of pencil stubs, paper clips, bits of worn-out blotting paper, and a ready reckoner with no covers. Of every one of these miscellaneous items a strict record had to be kept—"In case he gets off," Urry explained.

"And will he get off?" asked Manciple.

"Doubtful, very doubtful," said Urry. "Not with a cupboard full of stolen silver. Nice haul, that was. At a quick estimate I reckon it accounts for about sixteen unsolved robberies. Not unsolved, in a sense, because everything is unsolved until you solve it, and here we are."

"I'm very glad I was able to help you," Manciple said modestly. He had begun to wonder if his part in all this had been fully appreciated.

"Just so," said Blow. It was he, after all, who had sent for the Professor to be a witness in the first place.

"It is true that your ill-judged action precipitated our occupation of these premises," Inspector Urry said severely, "but you must not suppose, gentlemen, that we had not had them under close observation. We were not ready to move. As it is, there is now a real danger that we shall only round up the small fry, and that the mind directing this great criminal enterprize will escape us. To that, gentleman, we shall be brought by your 'help.' That is all."

"Do you mean we can go?"

"Certainly not. I have need of your assistance. It is of real value when properly channeled and controlled. I have almost finished here, and then we shall go on to a little party in the Mile End Road, for which, if I may suggest it, I think it will be advisable to assume a disguise. I should like you, Dr. Blow, to wear, if you will, a false mustache and eyebrows; and you, Professor—you have the figure for it—a black beard and a monocle.

You will look rather like a lady novelist of my acquaintance, but never mind."

Elkins said lugubriously from the outer room, "Nothing here, sir, except a lot of notebooks marked 'Supplied for the Public Service' but with nothing in them and a teaspoon marked 'J. Lyons.'"

"Well, you get off for a cup of tea and see if you can drop it unobtrusively before you come back. Not worth going through all the usual channels; it would take months. And I dare say we can use the notebooks—heaven knows our activities are undertaken in the public service. Only a fool would do it for the pay."

"Yes, sir."

"And don't quote me, Elkins."

"No, sir."

"Well, get off."

Dr. Blow wandered about the office, peering at this and that. The Professor sat looking at the floor, trying to envisage lady novelists and wondering if such a profession would suit Miss Emily Cakebread's talents.

Urry swept most of the junk off the desk top and back into the drawers, and then stood up. "Finished here," he said.

"What were you looking for?" asked the Doctor, picking up a copy of a reference given in 1937 by the Hon. Mrs. Paton-Hervey to one Bridget Briggs.

"I was looking for evidence," said the Inspector. "Evidence!"

"In other words," said Manciple, "he doesn't know." He brought out his wallet, and carefully extracted a charred slip of paper, which he laid before the Inspector. "Does this help, I wonder?" he said softly.

Inspector Urry said nothing for about half a minute, during which time he closely scrutinized the fragment with a magnifying glass. Then he grunted.

"Damn all use, that," he said, finally. "If I had the rest of it, it would be another matter. You know what this is? It's part of the correspondence between this office and that precious office of yours, Dr. Blow, where they're always on about the Princess Sophey of Gand. It's all over this bit of letter heading. Where did you get it, Professor?"

"Out of the grate. There's the rest of the ashes, still there. I suppose none of the charwomen is on the books long enough to do a bit on the side for Alf."

"I scraped them over before you came. All pulverized and perishing little use, unless you use soot to clean your teeth. An old-fashioned custom, that; I bet Sophey of Gand loves it. Well, let's get on. I want to flush that little lot in the Mile End Road, but I don't want them to suspect I am on my way. So you gents will provide a diversion and act as decoys, see? Hold them in play-like. Keep them talking, that's the thing. I bet you can manage that between you! I've got to fix warrants and enlist the help of the local force and get on to my Chief and so on; it all takes time. In films they just kick the door in and begin shooting, eh, Professor? But we have to proceed in proper order."

"Suppose Alf comes back here? He'll know the game is up."

"Alf won't come back. If he does, he will be detained. Alf never yet went within twenty yards of a door with a copper standing outside it. Besides, they'll have tipped him off. Us chaps can't come in a place and start routing around without the other tenants noticing. But tipping him off we're here is one thing; letting him know we're on our way to Mile End Road is quite another. They can't read our thoughts and nor can he. He doesn't know we're on to Mile End Road—not yet. That's a little surprise for him."

"I am quite excited, Inspector. And what do you wish Professor Manciple and me to do?"

"Behave suspiciously, sir. You can do it, never fear. Go there, and if possible make your way in. Hear and see what you can, and then confront them. Spin the discussion out. By then we shall arrive."

"And why must we wear false whiskers for that, Inspector?" Manciple inquired, pursuing to the last his prejudice against dressing up.

"Because this is a diversion, sir, a feint. Every device helps to further delaying tactics. Good heavens, if I were not too busy I'd put one on myself and a wig as well! Police work may be mostly dull routine, but there's romance in it as well! Elkins would tell you, if he were here."

"And another thing," Manciple went on, ignoring all this. "What happens if they turn on us? Look at Mrs. Sollihull, Flash Elsie, and she was one of themselves. I pay taxes to be protected, not to be pushed into dangerous situations. I can just see myself being buried in a false beard and half my friends not coming to the funeral because they don't know it's me."

"The danger is small, Professor. Murder is not a habit, even with the hardened criminal. They would be more likely to tie you up and put you in a cupboard . . ."

"—probably a drafty one, at that. . . ."

". . . but I think I can promise you you will come to no permanent harm. And now tell me, Professor, what makes you think Flash Elsie was murdered by her associates?"

"Well, if they didn't, who did?"

"That's one of the things I am still trying to find out. And I expect to go some way further toward succeeding during the interesting course of this afternoon."

"Then I have only one thing more to say: Who pays for these foolish disguises and where do we get them?"

"The authorities will bear the cost, sir, but I must ask you not to lose them, especially the monocle. And I have everything you will need here in my pocket, including the spirit gum. Hell! The cork's come out!"

18

To Professor Manciple's mind, Dr. Blow entered too much into the spirit of the thing, especially as a bushy mustache and tinted glasses were at best only a concession to concealment and not a really effective disguise. For something spectacular in this department it was necessary to turn to the Professor, whose beard would have been a credit to W. G. Grace, except that perhaps W. G. Grace would not have worn it lopsided.

Before they had reached Aldgate the Doctor had begun saying "Hist" and putting his finger mysteriously to where he conceived his lips to be. Manciple's admonitory mumbles were vain and also unintelligible and their only effect was to make the conductress consider putting him off the bus. Fortunately, almost any eccentricity of appearance and behavior may be practiced with impunity in London, where the commonest reaction to any departure from the norm, whether by way of bare feet in November or eating pods of raw garlic out of a twist of *Pravda*, brings "Bloody foreigner" and a tolerant shrug. Despite this metropolitan indulgence, Dr. Blow was inviting attention by going down the last hundred yards of the Mile End Road practically on all fours. Manciple only staved off comment by saying loudly at intervals, "You dropped them just about here!"

The two detectives—for so they now thought of themselves—came to a halt by the mailbox for a council of war. The house they had under observation stood quiet and seemingly deserted, no smoke from the chimneys, no lights, no doors or windows open, no sound from within. But it was not really weather for fires, yet, and it was certainly not dark, and not everyone likes fresh air or considers that of the Mile End Road to be salubrious anyway; and, if you move about in carpet slippers and speak in undertones, very little noise will reach the street. All this Manciple explained to Blow, and Blow agreed.

"We could tie a piece of string to the knocker and pull it and run away," Blow suggested. "They always open the door and put their heads out then. At least they always did when I was a boy in Buxton."

"We didn't come here to run away," Manciple pointed out.

"Do they own the whole house?" the Doctor wondered. "Because if not, we could make out we were calling on someone else. I could open the front door, and if anyone came and said anything, we could say it was Mrs. Harris we wanted or Fred Aikin. I've made those names up, you know. Of course, if nobody came, then we'd be in and we could hide."

"Or we could say we had come to read the meter."

"It's too great a risk, Manciple. What if the real one came while we were doing it? Besides, they wear peaked caps."

The house certainly *looked* deserted.

"Oh, come on!" said the Professor. "After all, we are in disguise. We can be looking for lodgings. Let's go boldly up to the door and knock, eh?"

"You speak, then. You have an aptitude for this work which I find astonishing and admirable, although I pull your leg sometimes, my dear fellow. It is idle to skulk here; at any moment someone may wish to post a letter."

With this, they moved boldly forward, passed the three intervening houses, and mounted the five steps between peeling Corinthian pillars which led to the front door. Here, they paused. There were four bells, three of them labeled, and it was a question of choice.

"Basement, no name. Better not try that anyway. Ground floor, Isaacs; I don't suppose they let rooms."

"We don't actually want rooms, remember. They would be the ones to try, in that case. I couldn't *live* here, Manciple. Don't forget that."

"First floor, Lawless. Ha! ha! I bet they're respectable enough.

No, let's try the second floor, it takes them longer to come down and we can be thinking what to say. Second floor, Mrs. Tickler. Here goes."

"Are we looking for a room or rooms? And we must decide what food we need supplied. Good heavens, I haven't applied for digs since I came down from Oxford. It doesn't look as if it has a bathroom, Manciple, and they have to carry the dustbins out through the front door. We must say we must think it over; don't be precipitate."

The front door opened. "Yes?"

"Mrs. Tickler, madam?"

"Left last October."

"It says on the bell . . ."

"None of my business what it says on the bell. Mrs. Tickler left, and good riddance, last October; if you're her Tom she was always on about I'm sorry for you."

"My name is Gideon, madam, and I am not acquainted with Mrs. Tickler; had I been, it would not have been necessary for me to ask you if you were she when you opened the door."

"Just so," said Dr. Blow, nodding.

"Well, I'll just say good morning and sorry you been troubled. *I* don't mind traipsing up and down, up and down. Oh, no." The door closed.

"I think it was a man," Dr. Blow said, "that's why he was angry."

"Nonsense," Manciple answered, "they all wear caps and smoke pipes."

"Well, be that as it may, we are still outside and it will seem suspicious if we ring the bell again. We are to some extent protected from observation by the porch. You must shin up and go in through the fanlight."

"You are the thinner."

"But I am the less active. Indeed, I sometimes wonder if I have not allowed myself to get into a sedentary rut over the past thirty or forty years. I really very seldom take a walk now, and I much doubt if I have shinned up anything since we put those items on the Sheldonian in Greats Week, '98. Well, well, I will try. 'This he courageously invaded, and, having entered, barricado'd; ensconc'd himself as formidable as could be underneath a table . . .'"

"Hurry up," said Manciple, cutting all this short. "We're not in yet."

There was a curved glass fanlight over the door and it was already open about an inch—enough for the Doctor to insert his fingers and push. With a creak, the hinges gave and the fanlight slid along its iron groove. Manciple, supporting Blow on his shoulders, could see very little, but he felt the Doctor's weight increase and then lessen as he sprang—or, rather, shuffled—into the air and forced his body through the opening. A shower of dust and grit went down Manciple's neck. Inside the house there was a startling crash as the Doctor landed partly on a bamboo hall stand, and then the door opened and Manciple slipped inside.

"Good work!" he whispered.

"Yes," the Doctor replied. "Mind you, it wasn't locked, and that helped."

Despite the crash the house remained quiet. No doors opened. No angry voices called. The person from the second floor remained aloof, perhaps because it was a community hall stand in which she had no vested interest. The two detectives tiptoed toward the basement stairs and stood a moment listening at the top. Darkness below and no sound. Also a slightly dank smell, as if wet serge were piled in one corner.

Even Manciple now was prepared to say "Hist." His whisper was as conspiratorial as Blow's, his manner—had anyone been watching—quite as suspicious. Stair by stair, with infinite caution, they descended.

There were three rooms down there and a passage with a door opening into an enclosed yard, containing one sycamore tree and a great deal of lather which had overflowed from the drain when someone had poured away their washing-up water.

"No way out!" whispered Blow. "Unless you went up the tree."

The back room was a kitchen, very dark and damp. Empty.

The middle room, commanding from one grimy window a

broad perspective of the yard and the sycamore tree, was more or less empty. A broken-down armchair upholstered with green velvet had fungus growing on it.

Blow closed the door. "I should think they only use that room at Christmas," he murmured, "unless they go to a hotel."

The front room they approached with special caution. It was their last chance of being caught red-handed, and they wanted to be awake to every move. This room, from previous experience, they knew to be the one in common use. Even now, Alf might be crouching behind the door with a gun or a razor in his hand.

"Shall we push it open and creep in, or burst it open and wait for them to rush out?" asked Manciple, his hand on the knob.

"Just go in naturally," Blow said, ignoring the essentially unnatural element of their enterprise, "and if anyone says anything, say you are looking for the Ticklers. After all, their name is on the bell even if they did leave last October."

Professor Manciple opened the door. The room was empty, empty of people, that is. There was no lack of furniture. There was a large double bed with iron head and foot and brass knobs, a Chesterfield, and two easy chairs, several small chairs. The big cupboard Inspector Urry had promised them, a built-in affair beside the fireplace, and tables and sideboard and other trifles were there. This, obviously, was the inhabited part of the establishment, the only part that did not reek of damp. Here, it might even be possible to be comparatively snug, Blow thought, peering in. It was dark, being well below the pavement level, but they didn't dare light the gas jet. So they made a place for themselves in the big cupboard, among rugs and old clothes and other effects, and then sat one each side of the cold fireplace to await events. No good getting into the cupboard too soon; it wasn't inviting enough for that.

An hour passed, and then they heard a car draw up outside. Several people clumped up the front steps, which were directly outside and above the window of the room.

"Dive!" said Manciple, leading the way.

Less than a minute later three people entered the room.

Manciple and Blow could see nothing, but they heard the voices clearly enough. Alf first, then the boy, James Bernard Shaw—if that really was his name—and then a woman's voice, the voice of Miss Fisk.

Alf was already giving orders as they entered the room. "Jim, put the cases there. We've got about twenty minutes. Here, nip down to Rice's—it's after three, you'll have to go to the side door—and get two bottles of stout. Hurry!"

The door slammed, and Manciple sensed that the other two were now alone.

Miss Fisk was speaking. "Alf, can't you be serious? What do we want with bottles of stout? Twenty minutes, you say—ten's nearer the mark—and what must you do but tipple."

"Steady, little flower! I just wanted to get the boy out of the way. No need for him to know everything, is there, silly? Now you pop them ingots into the small case out of from under the kitchen sink while I tidy up here."

Again the door opened and shut. Alf began to whistle between his teeth, pulling out drawers and opening cupboards, but, luckily, not the big cupboard. That, obviously, was used only for clothes and so on, and Alf's preoccupation was with paper. He was burning correspondence, and once more Manciple's gorge rose at the thought; but he restrained himself. He whispered under his breath into Blow's ear, "They're packing up!"

Another car—a taxi, for Manciple heard the little ping of the meter bell—and another sound of clumping feet. A man's voice on the stairs. And then a silvery laugh. Manciple almost fell forward out of the cupboard in his efforts to see.

Blow said irritably, "Take your elbow out of my face! Is it the Inspector?" and Manciple answered shortly, "No. Keep quiet, if you want us to get out of here alive. It's that sailor they call 'The Greek.' I can see his earrings."

"He's the one that did it, you mark my words," Blow answered in his piercing whisper.

"Hist!" said Professor Manciple, finally succumbing to the magic of the word.

Alf was speaking again, and the thing was apparently a council of war. "Simple enough," he was saying, "we got to scram.

Gunstein phoned through, the Rozzers are swarming in Greek Street. It can't be more than a matter of time before they're on to this place, though I think we're in the clear a bit longer. They don't know about it, but they'll find out. 'The Greek's sailing tonight and I'm going with him. Ellie's going back to welfare work for a few months, and Jim's got a place with Lord Caburn —second footman, but with prospects. He ought to do well; he went with smashing references. So we share out and split up and meet again after Easter at Laura's. She'll move, of course, but you can all get the address from the boards."

"Not the address," said a voice that sent little shivers along Dr. Blow's spine, "only the telephone number."

"Now we got to clear or 'The Greek' and I will miss our train and it's the only one that catches the tide. Everybody's share is all worked out; less than was expected, because the Rozzers got a haul at Greek Street, but a decent bit. Jim—where the hell's that boy?"

"You sent him for stout."

"Laura, look after it. One thousand pounds, six. It's all counted out. Cocoa tin, Jim's lot. Laura, eighteen hundred pounds, three and seven. Got fivepence, love? Ellie, three thou—flat. 'Greek,' you got yours. Mine's in the case."

"Case is bloody heavy," Laura remarked, apparently lifting it.

"It's got the alarm clock in as well," Alf explained patiently. "Right, everybody? Split up, then. Laura, you better wait behind and wash up. Ellie, take a cab. Me and 'The Greek' will go by bus."

"I think they are going," Blow whispered in the darkness. "It was that that we were sent here to prevent. What had we better do?"

The voices were receding in the passage. Manciple made up his mind.

"Stay here in reserve," he whispered, "and let me see what I can do first. I'll make up some yarn."

Without waiting for a reply he pushed open the cupboard and stepped into the room, leaving Blow still concealed.

The Professor ran up the stairs two at a time. Already Alf

and "The Greek" were out on the pavement. Miss Fisk was in the hall, adjusting her hat. Laura had vanished.

"Oi!" cried the Professor, saying the first thing that came into his head. "I'm the new rent collector. You never gave notice, gentlemen. You forfeit the lease!"

Alf put down the heavy suitcase and said in a nasty voice, "What lease?"

"The Greek" took out a heavy, broad-bladed knife.

Miss Fisk pulled out one of her long hatpins.

Jim came round the corner carrying two bottles of stout.

19

Some magnetic compulsion drew the players in our drama together into a tight little knot, closely resembling a group of
basketballers gathered to throw at a goal; and Professor Manciple,
who was in the middle, kept bobbing up and down rather like
the captain and top-scorer of some redoubtable team, except that
he was saying in a high voice over and over, "I shall appeal to
the Confederation of Estate Agents and Auctioneers," and he had
his feet permanently off the ground. The whole company disappeared back into the house and the door slammed. From within,
an angry buzz might have been heard, and, suddenly, a dark
sticky liquid began to make its way under the door and down
the steps, giving out a strong odor of stout.

Professor Manciple, his arms pinioned behind him, was being
forced down the stairs. He was no longer saying anything, because in the engagement the greater part of his beard had been
pushed into his mouth. In his eyes was a wild light far fiercer
than ever illumined those of even the most zealous rent collector.
A long red scratch went down one cheek.

The only other casualty had been the bottle of stout, but Alf
was breathing hard and Miss Fisk rattled slightly as she walked.
Her blouse was full of loose wooden beads.

When they were all back in the basement room Alf said, "It's
that perishing perfesser."

"Professor Manciple, yes," Miss Fisk agreed. "I suppose that
means Dr. Blow is snooping around somewhere, the old idiot."

"He was hiding behind the mailbox," said Manciple, with ready
resource, spitting out a great tangled mass of beard. "He'll have

156

gone for help by now."

"If he doesn't get lost on the way!"

"You must not underrate Blow, Miss Fisk. He is a very able fellow, though naturally his immediate aptitude is not for physical action. He's sedentary, but shrewd when roused. He . . ."

"Shut up!" said "The Greek." He flourished his knife; already its bright blade was streaked and stained, though only with stout. "I'll slice you," said "The Greek."

"Place is like a bloody debate," Alf said, darkly. "Tie him to a chair and let's get off!"

With the aid of the Professor's necktie, a thick piece of cord, and a length of elastic, the prisoner was secured to his chair and once more the company prepared to separate.

Miss Fisk went first, saying, "I shall borrow Mr. Isaacs's bicycle." The boy Jim followed, rattling his cocoa tin cheerfully and singing under his breath, "Lord Caburn, here I come." "The Greek" reluctantly sheathed his knife.

"Right?" said Alf. "Right! Off we go. I suppose somebody will find him in the end."

Manciple, savoring without relish the novel experience of being gagged with an elastic garter, said nothing, but his eyes held an awful eloquence. He was discovering the seamy side of police work, and beginning to appreciate the lost tranquillity of numismatics.

Miss Fisk, cutting the corner fine as she pedaled for Aldgate, was almost overthrown by the big black police car sweeping into the turn. With a remark which the minister would have found disturbingly out of character the lady increased her pace, bending over the handlebars and half-rising from the saddle. The carpet bag bouncing and bobbing round her neck dribbled pound notes, which danced and fluttered behind her like the elements in some wild paper chase. On the whole, Miss Fisk's passage brought a breath of pleasurable excitement to the Mile End Road.

At the next corner the police car narrowly missed Alf, who was hurrying across to the bus stop, and "The Greek," who had put two heavy suitcases down in the middle of the road while he hitched up his trousers. He was beginning to regret the bit of cord now confining Professor Manciple to his hard kitchen chair.

The car surged past Rice's just as Jim went in with one empty stout bottle to collect fourpence.

And at number eight hundred and fourteen it skidded to a stop and policemen of all sizes began to spill out.

The lady who lived behind the bell marked Tickler looked out and scowled. "Why can't they go somewhere else and make their bloody films?" she asked. A little animation came into her voice, and she peered closer through her discreetly drawn curtains. "I wonder if any of them's Jack Hawkins. . . ."

Inspector Urry rang the bell marked Basement. Nothing happened.

Then he rang the ground-floor bell. Nothing happened.

The bell marked Tickler. Nothing happened, except that in the second-floor front somebody said, "Go and chase yerself."

"Right, Elkins!" said Urry, "through the fanlight."

Two minutes later the whole company was pouring down the stairs, except the man who had stayed behind to help Elkins out of the ruins of the bamboo hall stand.

The back room was empty. The middle room was empty. The door of the front room opened four inches, and then refused to move further.

"What the devil now?" asked Urry, striking a match in the gloom and trying to see in. "Here, you—the thin one—can you get your neck round the door?"

The thin one tried and at last said in a strangled voice, "It's a chair, sir, wedged under the door knob, with somebody sitting in it."

"Well, tell them to get up!"

"Sir, I can't get my neck back out!"

"You inside there! It's the police. The game's up! Come out!"

The thin policeman was now out of the action because by pulling frenziedly on the bottom rung of the chair he had shut the door on himself. Another policeman was trying to get in from the street through the window, but he was hampered by one of the bars of the grating which he had forced aside. It had got somehow under his belt. Urry's temper was rising. "Push!" he kept shouting through the keyhole to the thin constable, at the same time dodging the man's feet, which were flailing about in the passage. The situation was becoming absurd.

And then, with a convulsive wriggle, Manciple stood up, dragging the chair with him. The handle flew off the door, the door fell open, and Inspector Urry entered with the involuntary precipitation which is one of the hazards of police work in the field. The thin policeman's nose began to bleed, which was just as well, for otherwise he was in grave danger of a stroke.

Urry said, "Flown, by God. Another wasted warrant!" and sat down on the Chesterfield.

Professor Manciple moved across to him on all fours, still hampered and confined and with a very red face and angry eyes. He had passed ten extremely discouraging minutes and he was accumulating things to say as soon as the Inspector took off the gag.

Wearily, for this wasn't the kind of work he had come for, Inspector Urry bent and began to loosen the gag. An elastic gag is volatile and unpredictable. This one freed itself all of a sudden and caught the Inspector sharply in the eye.

"Don't cut the ropes!" Manciple said in an excited croak, "it's my necktie."

There was the untying of the bonds. The kitchen chair rattled to the floor, and Professor Manciple rose from his crouching position and began to rub various affected parts. He was dirty and disheveled, but conscious of having held the fort, such as it was.

"So they're gone!" said Inspector Urry.

"You must have passed them," Manciple said "a big, fat man with earrings. Alf, the boy they call Jim carrying a cocoa tin, and Miss Fisk. They haven't been gone two minutes. Most ingenious the way they wedged the door with my chair after they were outside. I thought you'd never get in. It was to delay you, of course. They sail on tonight's tide, all except the boy—he's gone for a footman—and Miss Fisk—she's going to lie low and do welfare work again. By the way, did you meet Laura? Bless my soul, and where's Blow?"

159

"Here I am," said a voice. "You said to stay in the cupboard."

"You don't need to stay in there *now*," said Manciple, irritably. "You could have come out and opened the door when the Inspector arrived and saved an infinite amount of bother. What the devil were you playing at, Blow?"

The only answer was a slivery laugh.

For the next two or three hours events moved too swiftly for Blow and Manciple really to keep abreast of them. First came the ride in the police car back to the West End, Urry and the two old gentlemen in the back and Elkins squeezed in beside the driver with Laura between them. All the other policemen had been given tasks at Mile End Road, to guard and search and collect fingerprints, and so forth.

At New Scotland Yard, Urry went in for a long time, leaving the others sitting in the car. He had to make alternative arrangements for rounding up the gang—and one of the hardest things to find in London is a middle-aged woman riding a man's bicycle. At last the Inspector reappeared. "Victoria!" he said, briefly. "We'll go home."

"I don't live at Victoria," Laura remarked, taking her hand off Elkins' knee in order to pat a curl into place against her cheek.

"You will come with us," Urry said severely.

"I don't mind," Laura said, putting her hand back on Elkins' knee.

Urry had telephoned from Scotland Yard for a car to meet their train, and as they left the station he asked Dr. Blow if he wished to be taken home. Blow said he thought so. The car turned into Priory Place and drew up at number ten.

"I think I'll get out here," Laura said sweetly. "Unless I'm under arrest?"

This was awkward. As it happened, Urry had no evidence against this one—not yet. There was a pause, then Dr. Blow said, "Perhaps I may offer you a cup of tea?"

"Let's all have a cup of tea," Manciple suggested.

"Elkins, you go back with the car and bring me any reports that have come in since the morning. Cut along, and look sharp. Thank you, sir, I think I shall enjoy a cup of tea."

Rather to Professor Manciple's surprise, Dr. Blow's study looked just the same as when they had left it nearly twelve hours ago. Here, time had stood still and events had made no impact—a very different state of affairs from that in that dreadful basement. Manciple had no further ambition to visit the Mile End Road.

Laura sat on the sofa, being the only person present who was unaware of the nature of its suspension, and Manciple took the chair which creaked, because then at least he knew in advance when the creaking might be expected. Inspector Urry found a seat and Dr. Blow hurried away to arrange for the cup of tea, which, presently, Miss Angell brought in on a tray. She had her street coat on, but nobody commented on this; she was obviously either going out or coming in, and what did it matter?

"Now, gentlemen," said Urry, "I think we will have a few explanations. And you, young woman, keep a still tongue in your head, and if Dr. Blow will permit, you may pour out the tea. If you aren't under arrest, you jolly soon will be unless you look out."

"I know my rights," said Laura. "Oh, well, here goes. How many lumps, Inspector?"

Inspector Urry began a careful review of the state of things.

"You think the thing starts with Flash Elsie being stabbed in your flat," he said, addressing Dr. Blow but taking Manciple in with a glance. "Nothing of the kind. That's where it finished. It all began some years ago when Alf Carter came out of the jug after doing five years for larceny. Alf was clever and in five years a man can do a good deal of thinking, if he's got the time on his hands. He'd worked out a perfect scheme. He began by taking over a perfectly genuine domestic servants' agency called Cooks and Butlers; the old boy who ran it, a quite respectable party, wanted to retire, and he knew cooks and butlers were on their way out. He sold the good will to Alf, and no doubt thought he had done well for himself. So he had, but he had also done well for Alf.

Alf builds up a team of bogus servants who are trained in larceny. Large hauls of silver and other valuables begin to be made, and the police are baffled. I admit it. These housekeepers and footmen and the rest don't disappear with bundles of swag. They stay at their jobs. It's only the swag that disappears."

"Hidden in the mattress!"

"Hidden in the mattress or some place. Then, when the housekeeper, or whoever it is, is in full view with a cast-iron alibi and can't possibly be involved, somebody sneaks in and carts the stuff away."

"Miss Fisk."

"Miss Fisk. Probably on a bicycle. She sends the stuff or takes it to Greek Street, where young Jim, who's a bit of a dab at chemistry, melts it down. Mind you, I'm telling you all this because I want to get it clear in your minds, because you already know or suspect some of it. We, in the police, have known it for months; we were just waiting to pounce."

"But so far as Mrs. Sollihull was concerned, somebody else pounced first?"

"Just so. I'm coming to that. Now, the boy Jim melts the stuff down, and 'The Greek' carts it away in his ship to Amsterdam or to whatever port he happens to be sailing to. Any of the great continental ports would do—Marseilles, Hamburg, Alexandria even. Silver ingots are an international currency."

"Pooh!" said Laura.

"Pooh, young lady? What do you mean, pooh?"

"Nothing, Inspector. I was just blowing on my tea."

"Just let it get cool in the ordinary way, Miss, like anybody else, will you? Where was I now? Yes, so that was the set-up, and over the course of a year or two they brought it to a fine art, and in order not to have to cut in too many people with shares, they gradually reduced the staff. In the end Flash Elsie was the only inside operator, and Miss Fisk did all the outside work. Jim melted down. 'The Greek' got rid of the stuff. And Alf did the office work. Simple as that."

"So what are you holding me for?"

"The charming Miss Laura. I'm coming to you shortly. Meanwhile, you can be drinking your tea, Miss, it's cool now."

Dr. Blow said suddenly, "Very nice. But who murdered Mrs.

Sollihull?"

"Not *who* murdered her, sir. That comes later. *Why* was she murdered, that's what I need to know. *Why?*"

"I suppose somebody disliked her, Inspector. And now I come to think of it, she did not appear a very lovable woman."

"Perhaps not, sir. But that's no excuse for murder—or would you think so?"

"Murder is quite inexcusable," Dr. Blow acquiesced, "especially in my house. That's the vexing thing. Here was this woman, almost a stranger, and somebody comes in . . ."

The telephone rang.

"Excuse me," said Urry, "that will almost certainly be Elkins. May I?" He answered the call and said, "Yes, yes," and then, "good." Then he rang off.

"They've got Miss Fisk," he announced, returning. "She's in the cells at Savile Row, accused of stealing a bicycle. Apparently she neglected to ask Mrs. Isaacs if she could borrow Mr. Isaacs' machine. Good, things are moving."

"Perhaps she asked Mr. Isaacs," Blow said, unwilling to leave any loophole unconsidered. "Doing six months," Urry answered briefly.

"They've also got young Jim," the Inspector went on. "Picked him up at Caburn Court cleaning the silver. Forged references. Lord Caburn was lucky that time; the boy hadn't got his furnace installed!"

"I think it's wicked," said Laura. "He was only cleaning it after all, and isn't that what footmen are for? He tries to go straight, and what do you do but hound him? Forged references, my foot! As if it mattered. As a matter of fact, they were genuine. He only rubbed out the other chap's name."

"Alf and 'The Greek' have sailed, which suits me fine. They'll be at sea three days, and I hope Alf's seasick. Then they'll be arrested as they go ashore at Brest."

Inspector Urry drank his tea; it needed no blowing upon.

"Manciple," Dr. Blow said an hour or two later, when the Inspector had gone, "I can understand your preoccupation with more important matters during the temporary excitement of the chase, but don't you think that now you might tuck your shirt in at the waist and take off the wires that were holding your false beard. You look bizarre, my dear fellow."

"I feel bizarre, Blow. The day has been a strain. All you did was skulk, and whatever else you did, in a cupboard. I have been tied to a chair, gagged with a lady's garter, stabbed, and bathed in stout. It would be something if I didn't look bizarre."

"I thought a bizarre was where they sold things," Laura observed. She was curled up, very much at home, on the sofa. The establishment pleased her, as a change from the normal. Naturally, if she had to see much of it, there'd have to be something done about all the silly, dusty books. But nobody could deny that it was refined.

"Dear me," said Dr. Blow at this, "I had forgotten the young lady. What is to be done with her? I have no accommodation here for guests, unless Miss Angell—but that would be unfair. No three-foot bed can be expected to accommodate two ladies and a parrot. I must ask you, Miss Laura, to go to an hotel. I have heard good reports of the Wilberforce Temperance . . ."

"The Wilberforce Temperance, oh my God!" said Manciple distractedly.

"My dear fellow, whatever is the matter?"

"Miss Emily Cakebread! I forgot all about her! She's down there sitting, waiting for me with a tin trunk."

"Surely, after so very full a day, you do not propose attending an assignation at this hour, Gideon? You are no longer a young man, remember. Telephone to the hotel; ask Miss Cakebread to excuse you; and at the same time reserve a room for Miss Laura. That is the wisest plan."

"A temperance hotel sounds sweet, but Willie dear . . ."

"Quite impossible."

Professor Manciple reached for the telephone. "I shall leave a message; I shall say I have been detained . . ."

"You may be yet, at that," said Laura.

20

One thing was quite clear in the Chief Constable's mind: he didn't care for cases of murder. It entailed too much office work. Here he was, in his office again on a beautiful sunny morning.

Urry didn't like murder cases either. Six hours' sleep on Friday, bisected by a telephone call at 5:00 A.M.; and four last night. Hard at it all Saturday afternoon, which probably explained why the Rovers had lost three-nothing.

Elkins, on the other hand, rather enjoyed the excitement of driving about in the car and taking things down. Twice already he had been mentioned in the local paper—once as Elvings, it's true, but that wouldn't count against him. Elkins had his own theories—they changed from day to day—and he didn't despair of making a sensational arrest or at any rate a disclosure. Then his promotion might be back-dated even further.

So the Chief Constable looked peevish; Urry looked disgruntled; and Elkins wore an air of unwonted brightness—when they all met to discuss the Mile End Road adventure.

"Take that grin off your face, Elkins," said Inspector Urry, restoring the status quo.

"Now then," said the Chief Constable, looking at the clock, "let's begin. All here? Er—Urry . . . ?"

"They're all either in the bag or on tap, sir," the Inspector began. "The boy Shaw is under arrest. He's at Lewes, but they'll send him on to us. Fisk is at Savile Row, stealing a bicycle . . ."

"Stealing a bicycle at Savile Row, Urry?"

"Stealing a bicycle's the charge, sir; we can make it stick. Then we can get the more serious charge worked out at our leisure—

not that we have much leisure, sir. Alf Carter and 'The Greek' are in a freighter on their way to Brest; we'll pick them up on arrival."

"Yes. If you'd arrested them before they went, we wouldn't have had to pay their fares home. Well, never mind, perhaps it can't be helped; but it's no use you and Elkins saying you want a trip to Paris."

"The minor people are under observation, sir. That girl, Laura, and her associate, Millie; but, quite honestly, I can't see any suitable charge right now. They never did more at most than carry messages and things like that."

"I hope you can do better with Shaw than charging him with fetching two bottles of stout after hours."

"Oh, yes sir. The electric furnace is in his name, plain enough, and four installments still to pay."

"Good. Now, Urry, we've done a good job for the London boys, breaking up this little lot for them; but it's none of our business, really. What we want to know is, *who killed Flash Elsie?* Hey?"

"I know, sir. I've been thinking about that."

"Thinking! This is no time for thinking, Urry. You want to get some results. Was it Dr. Blow? Was it this Manciple? Fisk? It wasn't suicide, was it?"

"No sir. She'd have needed to be a contortionist. No, it wasn't suicide nor accident. It was murder; but was it premeditated murder or a spur of the moment job? That's my problem. Premeditation means a sort of permanent motive, if you see what I mean. Impulse might arise spontaneously from some trivial quarrel."

"Well, you've had two or three weeks to decide."

"Yes sir. And I have decided. I feel sure it was premeditated. A quarrel, a sudden blow means noise. And that Dr. Blow couldn't possibly be so wrapped up in his silly poems not to hear that in the next room. But if Elsie were entertaining a familiar guest and they were chatting in ordinary low tones—and then he ups and stabs her, that could be done quite unobtrusively. He sneaks out—she, if you like—leaving the body like we found it."

"It was found with a knife in the back. Why not take the knife along? Incidentally, what were the prints again?"

166

"The murderer left the knife so as to cast suspicion on somebody else, as I see it, sir. And somebody else, who didn't care to
have suspicion cast on him or her, came along afterward and carried the knife off. As for prints, there were none to correspond
with a stabbing grip. Finger and thumb where Professor Manciple originally picked it up by the top of the haft. Nothing on
the main haft except confused smudges—that's made of cor-
rugated plastic—one thumb print on the blade itself—Elkins'."

"Elkins! You don't think Elkins . . ."

"You can't stab someone by holding a blade with one thumb,
sir. Besides, Elkins was on duty that night, with me. And I assure you . . ."

"Come, come, Urry, don't take offense, man!"

"No sir. Well, so I see it like this. One, the murderer. Two,
the person the murderer wishes to implicate. Three, the implicated person, or another, who makes off with the weapon."

"Any one of these would point to the others. Even the one who
took the knife away ought to be charged as an accessory. Making
extra work for us. Yes."

"It's no trouble, sir," put in Elkins, anxious not to be thought
unzealous.

The others ignored him.

"Now, sir," Urry went on, "this is how I see it. Fisk is right in
the middle of the picture, and on top of that apparently she
runs up and down walls. That's suspicious in itself. But stabbing
isn't a woman's way, not with a sailor's knife. Carving knife on
impulse, yes—and I've known them break mirrors over people's
heads and things like that, but always in a passion, never in cold
blood. To go off with somebody else's knife concealed on the person and then bring it out and stab, no, I don't see it. Though,
mind you, Fisk is no ordinary female, I grant you that. So she
might have done it. Now, 'The Greek'. Well, of course to him,
stabbing would come natural. But why should he leave his own
knife or even anyone else's knife. Do the job and depart would
be his method. But the one who took the knife away wouldn't
be the one who did the job . . ."

"Why not, Urry? Maybe he forgot the knife first time and came back for it."

"You mean, someone like Dr. Blow, sir? But if he forgot it, he'd go on forgetting. The thing would be there to this day."

"Sir," said Elkins, " 'The Greek' had his knife with him yesterday, unless he's got two. He used it to knock the neck off a bottle of stout."

"You mean to say, Urry, you don't even know for certain that this knife you're holding belongs to 'The Greek'?"

"I'm morally certain, sir. After all, nobody is going to come forward and say, 'That knife you found sticking in the body belongs to me.' He had no knife when we first interrogated him, even if he's got one now; and this knife was found in the butter at that girl's flat; and we know 'The Greek' and she were associated; and we don't know any more sailors in that set up. Dammit, sir, if we don't assume something, we'll never get anywhere."

"Even assuming things, you don't seem to get far, Urry. Mind, I'm not blaming you. I know it's hard, uphill work—murder. Carry on."

"I think something like this, as a working hypothesis: an unknown does the stabbing, but 'The Greek' is the one that takes the knife away. That means someone trying to frame 'The Greek' and 'The Greek' not having any. It means he knows he's being framed, and it also means someone close enough to him to be able to get hold of his knife. Also, don't forget this, the unknown murdered Flash Elsie, so he or she also had a grudge against her. Now—motives. In a case like this, either money or passion. Not money, because they were all making a tidy bit—more than I make, sir, even with another penny on the rates! And Flash Elsie was the one that was bringing it in. Passion's another matter. Passion is irresponsible, unreasoning, wild. If Elsie and 'The Greek' were carrying on, and a third party . . ."

"Third party risk, eh, Urry! Ha!"

"Ha ha! sir, very good! I must tell my wife that. 'Third party,' I said, and the Chief Constable, quick as a flash . . ."

"Quite so, Urry. Yes. Well, get on." ('I said to Urry, "Third Party risk, eh, Urry . . ." ')

"Yes sir. And that points to Fisk."

"I thought Fisk was in love with this Alf Carter. According to Dr. Blow . . ."

"Dr. Blow, sir, was craning his neck through a grating and peeping in at a grimy window. What could he really see or know? They'd that minute arrived in the place; it isn't as if they were in bed or anything. He was probably helping her off with her coat. But mark this: Alf's name is Carter. And Flash Elsie called herself Mrs. Carter. She also called herself, or was called, Mrs. Cuttle. Carter for professional reasons; Cuttle from choice."

"Nobody would call themselves Cuttle from choice."

"They might if they were in love, *in love,* sir. Now, this fellow, 'The Greek,' he's entered in his paper as George James Cuttle. It's odd how often they keep the same Christian names. He's that fellow Gilstrap, naturally. And Fisk was in love with him before Flash Elsie came along. Her exact words are in the report—here, sir." Inspector Urry thumbed through the pile of papers on the Chief Constable's desk and began to read: " 'It was all understood between us, and then one day Elsie turned up . . .' Again, sir, here: 'George's head was turned . . . after that, it was never the same . . . we lost touch. . . .' "

"But she says he was a coal merchant."

"Well, sir, and now he's a stoker; same line of country, only sort of retail instead of wholesale."

"But I thought the fellow was a Greek; didn't somebody say he had rings in his ears?"

"It's a nickname. I've checked on all that. You remember Miss Fisk said he was 'superior'; she meant he had two-pennorth of education. So, in the stokehold he gets called 'The Greek' because he's got a smattering of learning and uses unlikely words and doesn't drop his aitches. They might have called him Doc or the Professor, but somehow they hit on 'The Greek.' Fisk says they lost touch during the war. That's when he first went to sea. After the war he took up with Alf through Elsie's introduction. We know all that now from the London inquiries. All the background stuff ties up. What we aren't quite clear on is Fisk's first contact with the gang, but we shall fill in the blanks. That rigmarole she told us was part-truth, part-lies. She was certainly companion to this old dowager, and the old girl left her about two pounds a week. At first, maybe Fisk could manage on that, with bits of odd jobs. Then, the cost of living began to rocket and she got behind with the rent—or whatever it was—and picked up with Alf's little lot. If she was going round stooging for Flash Elsie, she might have worked with them for ages before running into 'The Greek.' Then, at last, she must have met him and all the old feeling revived. But, by this time, he was carrying on with Flash Elsie full swing. So what does Fisk do?"

"What?"

"She stabs Elsie and frames 'The Greek.' Then, presumably, she goes back over the roofs. It was pure chance that Elsie had got a job next door; and, incidentally, so close to the port where 'The Greek' was, for most of the time he sails from London River."

"Well, it's a theory, Urry. See if you can make it stick."

"Yes sir. At least, it lets old Blow out. I'm getting quite fond of him."

"You don't think, Urry, that there was anything between him and Miss Fisk, or him and the housekeeper, or Manciple and the housekeeper, or Manciple and Miss Fisk?"

"Manciple's sweet on Emily Cakebread," Elkins put in.

"I don't know, sir," Urry admitted. "The only thing is to work on one theory at a time. But, of course, if anything doesn't fit, then we make a note of it and try it somehow else. Murder's a jig saw, sir; that's what it is."

"Well, cut along, Urry. Cut along."

Dr. William Blow moved uneasily in his chair, and a small frown appeared, deepening the already deep lines of his brow. He laid down his pen.

Dr. Blow knew at once the cause of his distress. He was getting used to this kind of thing. Dr. Blow was hungry.

Strange, that, all the same; for he had a perfectly satisfactory housekeeper, he remembered saying so last night. The woman was a treasure, so far as he remembered. Quiet about the house, very clean, civil, and unobtrusive. A parrot was unusual, perhaps, but the creature had given no trouble. But it was certainly ten o'clock, because Dr. Blow always worked for one hour before breakfast, beginning at nine. And he had begun at nine, he distinctly remembered, because nine was the time when he always began. And now he was hungry, so it must, of course, be ten. Just so.

Where, then, was his breakfast?

Dr. Blow laid down his pen and made for the kitchen. The fire was out and there was no sign of any meal in preparation. Nor was there any sign of Miss Angell. The Doctor moved from room to room in a way all too familiar, calling softly so as not to seem enraged—you can't be too careful not to offend them— "Miss Angell! Miss Angell!" Answer came there none. At last he paused, hesitating before the housekeeper's bedroom door.

Ought he to telephone Manciple?

But it wasn't like the middle of the night, no. At ten o'clock, when she ought to have been preparing his breakfast—when, indeed, it ought to be ready prepared—there could be hardly any imputation of impropriety in just gently tapping, and perhaps an interrogatory murmur at the door of "Miss Angell?" He could say he thought he heard cries of distress from the parrot and was it all right?

He tapped. He called. He ventured to turn the handle of the door. As if from established habit, his eye fell first upon the carpet. All was well—no blood, no body. Nobody, in fact. Not even a parrot. Miss Angell had gone.

It would be necessary, after all, to telephone Manciple.

Manciple was not, in the curious old phrase, "best pleased" at the interruption. They had agreed not to meet that morning. Blow had intended doing a little work, belatedly enough, on Samuel Butler; stimulated to this by a communication from the University Press. And Manciple had remembered the essential necessity for completing his paper on the coinage of King Canute. And now, here was Blow pouring out some nonsense about breakfast and parrots and no Angell in the house.

"Wait," said the Professor, "I'll come over."

They went into the housekeeper's room together. It was neat and tidy. Nothing amiss, except that the parrot cage was not in its customary place and there was a general air of emptiness which follows the packing and removing of personal knickknacks. Miss Angell was indubitably gone for good. Her letter said so, for she had left a letter:

Dr. Blow,

I have been obliged to leave your employment without giving the customary notice, although this course had been in my mind for several days. Tonight was the last straw. I have never been asked to wait upon a woman of the streets. If the girl is not a hussy, I don't know what she is, sitting like that showing her knees in front of three men. Besides, you are eccentric in your habits, Dr. Blow. In and out at odd hours. Today you never came back to lunch, and toasted cheese can't be kept hot indefinitely. So I must ask you to accept my notice and I shall leave at once. Any wages can be forwarded on through the Agency, or I don't care if you keep them.

Your obedient servant,
Doris Angell (Miss)

"I call that a very nice letter," Blow said. "I had no idea she wasn't satisfied. Of course, a woman like that wouldn't understand a police matter like the presence of Miss Laura, and, perhaps, I ought to have carried in the tray of tea myself. How vexing to have missed the toasted cheese yesterday, but I blame her for that. You ought never to toast cheese without first seeing if people are at home. It must be eaten at once, I agree. Well, Manciple, I must go round to Cakebread's and get another."

"I should like very much to go round to Cakebread's, Blow. Very much. Do you know, I have grave suspicions. Miss Cakebread appears to me something different from what she seems."

"What an extraordinary observation, Manciple. Surely, to *seem* is to seem, but you say . . ."

"Blow, suppose Miss Cakebread murdered Mrs. Sollihull? Wouldn't that explain everything?"

"Not to me, it wouldn't. It would, in fact, explain nothing. Why should Miss Cakebread murder Mrs. Sollihull? She never even met her; their communication, such as it was, was entirely conducted by card index."

"Listen, William. Why shouldn't Miss Cakebread murder her —someone did. Someone, did; that's the thing. Comparatively few people get murdered, by comparison with getting knocked over by a motorcycle or eating something that disagrees with them. Murder's the exception, and so the reason for it is, too. That Miss Cakebread is deep, you admit that much I suppose. All I said was, I'd like to go and see her."

"My dear fellow, as it happens, I have a reason for going to see her myself, so do come along. Miss Angell, you know; I must get another. No time like the present, except that I'm hungry. I think I must just make a cup of cocoa first. You don't think, do you, that my going in yesterday morning to make cocoa upset her? But *cocoa*, you know, if it isn't exactly made to the proper formula is quite undrinkable. One and one-third level teaspoonfuls . . ."

"Blow, make your cocoa, for heaven's sake, and come on! Er— I think perhaps a cup of cocoa . . . But you will excuse me, I know, if I just make my own. With cocoa . . ."

"Just so. Well, come along."

Twenty minutes later, fortified, the one by a thick syrupy brew and the other by a pale watery one, the two connoisseurs left Priory Place and made their way in a leisurely manner to Cakebread's. Only the sight of a great yellow rain cape flapping in the breeze outside the Surplus Stores prevented them walking past the place, for by this time they were deep in a discussion of the probable source material for Selden's *Titles of Honour*.

"Please enter" said the notice. Dr. Blow and Professor Manciple entered. Miss Cakebread was dictating; Miss Emily was taking down.

". . . and, of course, we are most gratified and delighted, dear Lady Orelebar . . . Oh, it is Dr. Blow, Emily. We will finish our correspondence later."

"Remember me?" said Manciple. "Lady Orelebar's second cousin. But I can attend by appointment if you like; in which case, let us make the appointment." He went slightly pink. "Er —my little joke, you know. I am accompanying the Doctor."

"If Miss Angell is dead," Miss Cakebread said, "I am afraid we shall have to close Dr. Blow's account."

"But, Christina . . ."

"Be silent, Emily. Good domestics are rare enough, without this quite unjustifiable prodigality of decease. In the ordinary way, when they leave, we get them back. But when they leave Dr. Blow they are withdrawn permanently from the labor market. It is unsatisfactory."

"Miss Angell is not dead," Dr. Blow said. "Not so far as we are aware. She has merely left my employment, taking her parrot with her, and, indeed, it would have been pointless for her to have left it behind. In this, at least, she displayed a nice consideration."

"She was very fond of Augustus."

"Yes, well, that is not pertinent. What is, is what about another?"

"I must make a sad confession, Dr. Blow. At the present time we cannot offer you another. We have no housekeepers at present on our books. I will, however, telephone to our associate agency, Cooks and Butlers of Greek Street . . ."

"Fat lot of good that will do," Manciple put in. "If anybody answers the phone it will be Elkins."

"The best governess I ever had on my books was called Elkins," Miss Cakebread said. "It must be all of forty-five years ago. Her Royal Highness . . ." She fell silent, musing on remembrance of things past.

"I cannot feel that there is much prospect of a satisfactory exchange just now with the Greek Street Agency," Dr. Blow observed, "but I have heard you speak in high terms from time to time of another associate agency in, I think, Torquay."

"Devon Domestics," Miss Cakebread agreed. "Yes. But just now they are closed for inventory."

"Inventory! Surely out-of-work servants are not stacked on shelves!"

"Devon Domestics sell pottery as a side line and do very well. It is quite surprising—I fear I am revealing professional secrets, but never mind, Dr. Blow is an old and valued customer—it is quite surprising how much pottery the servants supplied by Devon Domestics seem to break."

"At least that seems a more innocent racket than the Greek Street Agency's one," Professor Manciple remarked. He wondered what Miss Cakebread's racket was.

"Miss Cakebread," Dr. Blow said, "I must rely upon you to send me *somebody*. I can't live on cocoa, though it is a most nutritious drink."

"If all else fails," Miss Cakebread promised, "I will come myself."

Miss Emily Cakebread gave a little gasp, but Manciple interrupted any comment she had intended.

"Then that's settled," he said, cheerfully—it wasn't him to whom Miss Cakebread would be coming. "Now, look here, Miss Cakebread, Miss Emily Cakebread tells me you have turned her out of house and home, as well as giving her the sack. I suppose she's here this morning working out her notice. Well, it won't do. This is a family business, and Miss Emily is entitled to work in it by ties of blood and old association. In the same way, it's outrageous to send her off like that with a tin trunk to a temperance hotel. Miss Emily is no longer young . . ."

"Oh, Gideon!"

"I have already told her she'll never see forty again," Miss Cakebread said. "She's headstrong and foolhardy. But I have taken her back."

"I don't want to be taken back. I keep trying to tell you. Those two days at the temperance hotel were the happiest days of my life. I'm sick of writing letters to Lady Orelebar, especially as she never answers."

"If you mean my second cousin," Manciple observed, "she isn't likely to. She's been dead twelve years."

Miss Cakebread sank into a chair and wept.

"Just so," said Dr. Blow. " 'Tears, idle tears.' The death of a valued friend and client is always touching. But—twelve years? Surely some of those housemaids would have come back and told you?"

"Christina," Miss Emily said, "hadn't you better tell them?

That letter to Lady Orelebar, it was always the same one, when people came in. Just a blind to make us look busy. Dr. Blow, you were the only customer we had!"

"Exactly so," said Dr. Blow. "I knew there must be some reason why they came round so often with the account."

21

"For the moment," Inspector Urry said, "you will be charged with stealing Olly Isaacs' bicycle. There may be other charges later. Much will depend on how frank you are with me now."

"And how did Olly Isaacs get it, anyway. None of your two shillings a week and ride it away for him. He pinched it outside Fenchurch Street station, I can tell you that!"

"Miss Fisk, with your long association with welfare work and your extensive acquaintance with the ministry, you must well know that two wrongs don't make a right. At least, he wasn't caught pinching it outside Fenchurch Street station. But you were trailed all the way from the Mile End Road to Carlisle Street; and wherever Olly Isaacs got it from, he's burned his name under the saddle with a red-hot poker, so it's more his than yours. Now listen, my dear. Murder is what interests us, not stolen bicycles. Who did for Flash Elsie? Can you tell me that? If so, I'll jolly well buy you a bicycle myself!"

"How much do you know, Inspector?"

"Never mind how much I know; how much do *you* know, that's the thing."

"Alf didn't trust her. That's why I had to go round and collect the stuff, after she'd gathered it up and hidden it. Once before, she came back with a few bits of plate and he knew for a fact they had lashings of silver. Making a bit extra on the side. So I used to spy on her. I went from town to town, wherever she was working. Sometimes she stayed in a job six months, you know. You can't always pinch the stuff the night you move in. I never had to speak to her, and, indeed, I doubt if she knew me by sight. I hadn't had anything to do with her for years. Alf organized everything. I'd get the wire to collect, and it would be stuffed in the mattress. I'd go in through her bedroom window while she was serving dinner, and she'd never see me nor I her —not then. But, previously, I'd have kept an eye on the pawn-shops on her afternoon out, just so as she didn't try any double-cross. And one afternoon I saw them on the golf links together, her and Alf."

"Alf!"

"Yes, Alf. Just when I was beginning to care for him, she took him away. It was once too often!"

"So you killed her?"

"Certainly not, Inspector. That would have been most im-proper. I told Alf he could get somebody else, because I was through. And I asked Miss Cakebread to find me a situation. That was a day or two before the murder."

"And after the murder, you and Alf had a reconciliation?"

"Alf was certainly both contrite and considerate. We had it out and I agreed to stand by him. But not now, of course."

"Why not now?"

"I was thunderstruck yesterday when he said he was going off with 'The Greek' and with all those ingots. He double-crossed the lot of us. He must have gone off worth thousands! And leav-ing me to get away on a stolen bicycle. I tell you, he wanted me to be caught. He hoped I'd swing!"

Inspector Urry looked round the bare little room at Savile Row, with its frosted-glass window, its green paint and buff walls, its flat, rubber-tiled floor. He never felt at home in these London stations—too big, too clean, too impersonal. They'd lent him the room because Miss Fisk was on a local charge, nothing to do, yet, with Urry's main investigation. But he couldn't help thinking he'd have got more out of her in her own place or even at Dr. Blow's, which seemed to be her home away from home.

"Well," he said, finally, "I hope you won't swing. Of course, it would make the prospect even remoter if we knew who did, in fact, stab Flash Elsie."

"She died because . . ."

"Yes! Because . . ."

"Because she wouldn't play ball."

Inspector Urry had to leave it at that. Damned annoying! But he had left himself only about three minutes to get to Carlisle Street by three, and he mustn't be late because the Chief Constable was meeting him there. The Chief Constable had suddenly evinced a desire to see the terrain against which so much of the drama had been set, and he was making an informal tour of the principal beauty spots. That morning he had been down to the Mile End Road, escorted by Elkins. Most of the lunch hour he had passed train-spotting at Clapham Junction. And now, at three, he was going to have a look at the place where the knife was found, before going on to Greek Street for a quarter of an hour. Then he meant to have a quick one at Bamboni's, and catch the Belle back home.

Urry sighed, and said to the local man, "Lock her up again. I'll look in later."

The Chief Constable was standing with his coat collar turned up in an angle of the wall where Carlisle Street joined the square. As Urry drew near, the Chief Constable hissed, "Keep on walking. We're watched!"

Urry kept on walking and the Chief Constable followed. Discreetly, a little way behind, came Laura and Dr. Blow.

As Laura said, they must see these two out of sight before they nipped in; and the Chief Constable stuck out a mile. Blow scarcely understood all this, but he acquiesced. They were going into the flat to make a cup of tea, because Laura said she wanted to put her feet up and Millie wouldn't be in today before four, so there was plenty of time. Then they were going to collect one or two pieces of clothing and general oddments, and Laura was going to clear out. She'd been offered a nice job as receptionist at the temperance hotel, and she fancied a few weeks by the sea. Besides, temperance commercial travelers, the hotel's main clientele, interested her. They looked as if they needed telling how best to spend their money.

The two official detectives dived across Oxford Street and made for Rathbone Place.

"Now!" said Laura. "Cut back this way and we'll be there in a jiffy. Why look, here's Millie!"

Stepping lightly toward them came Millie—and Dr. Blow gave a strangled scream and dived into a lady's blouse shop, crying "Keep her off! Keep her off!" and blundered through a door into a cubicle in which someone was trying on a blouse two sizes too small. For a moment there was pandemonium, and by the time the Doctor had made profuse apologies and purchased a pink georgette blouse, Laura and her friend had disappeared. Shaken and disheveled, Dr. Blow took the next train home. After all these years, to encounter that Mrs. Hoptroft!

In the meantime Laura and Millie made their way back to the flat not much disturbed by the Doctor's disappearance. Laura knew where to find him again and Mrs. Hoptroft had no further interest in him.

"He's not a bit game," she warned Laura, "and he really hasn't much money. Laugh! There was I, that time, my dear, not a stitch on . . ."

"Well, I like him," said Laura. "He's a gentleman. And how many gentlemen do we meet in the profession?"

"I don't want to meet gentlemen. I go where the money is!"

They were destined to meet gentlemen, however, for already the tread of Inspector Urry and the Chief Constable could be heard on the stairs.

"Hell," said Laura, "they've tailed us. Well, we're doing nothing. Better take that picture of you off the wall and put up Liberace."

"Ah!" said the Inspector, unable just then to think of anything else.

"Come with a warrant, Inspector?"

"I am not preferring charges," the Inspector said, "but I will ask you, in the friendliest way, one or two questions.—And you, madam—Millie, I think is the name."

"Millie Hoptroft. You got nothing on me. I pay my fines in court and give no trouble."

"Why does Miss Ellen Fisk call for air when your name is

mentioned?"

"Is this a conundrum?"

"He means Ellie, Millie. You know, Alf's Ellie. The one who came here that night—well, it was morning really. Made herself a slice of toast and went to sleep in the armchair."

"I still don't know why she swoons. Perhaps she's subject to them."

"She came here *that* night—which night?"

"It would be a Wednesday, three or four weeks ago."

"And why would she come *here;* she's a lady having very little in common with you ladies."

"Well, you see, if ever Alf worked late he might come on here afterward, and so she went to Greek Street and it was locked up, then she came on here. Actually, Alf was inside that night; drunk, you know. He does, now and again, if excited."

"He was excited that night then. He got drunk. And he was inside."

"Yes. And Miss Fisk came on over, and when he wasn't here she said 'Oh well' or maybe it was 'Oh hell' and could she have a cup of tea. So I made her a cup of tea."

"*You* made her a cup of tea. And was Mrs. Hoptroft here?"

"Heavens, no! Afternoons is Millie's time, four till eight or so. Anybody could tell you that, everyone knows Millie because it's by daylight, you see. They don't know me 'cos I come on after the offices are closed and they've gone home."

"But she told me, next day, when I said whose knife was it in my butter."

"I've got it!" Inspector Urry said. "She didn't cry for air at the name of Millie—a natural mistake. It was Millie's *butter* that disturbed her. Bet you a quid, sir, she brought the knife."

"She brought it, all right. Why didn't you ask? Great heavy, nasty thing. It frightened the wits out of one of my gentlemen. I was glad to see it go."

"You'd have been gladder still if you'd known that that knife had done murder! Well, sir, nothing more here, I reckon. Let's get along, eh?"

"Thank you, ladies," the Chief Constable said gallantly, "for the insight you have given us into your interesting lives. Ahem! Good day."

"Four till eight any time," said Millie.

"So far, so good," Urry said. "I'm glad to have you with me, sir, you bring me luck. And you don't fidget, like Elkins. Well, that's another step forward. Fisk filched the knife. Why? Because it was 'The Greek's.' So she was protecting him. Who had it in for him, that's the next step. Alf, I suppose. You heard what she said; he gets drunk when he's excited. He got drunk that night; he was in the cells—we know that anyway. But what was he excited about. Eh?"

"You tell *me*, Inspector. Investigation is your department. I only administer."

"Well sir, it's really common sense. He knew Elsie was being fixed that night."

"But he didn't do it."

"Oh hell! Maybe he wasn't arrested till after. I must look up the trains. Could he have nipped down, done it, nipped back, got drunk, and got arrested in time? Savile Row'll know the time he was arrested."

"If he's in the clear, Urry, then what? Not Miss Fisk, obviously. She hid the knife thinking to protect the murderer. Thinking to protect 'The Greek,' like as not. I suppose it couldn't have been 'The Greek' after all. That business of going to the pictures isn't any sort of alibi."

"But he was really in Gravesend, sir. We've established that. Miss Fisk either wouldn't have used his knife or she'd have left it. She wouldn't use it and leave it and then pop back for it as an afterthought. I've assumed—you'll forgive me assuming—that it was a crime of passion and jealousy. Don't forget this Laura occasionally calls herself Carter. What was her position, so far as Alf goes? Not his daughter; they always send them to good schools and keep it dark about being crooked. Laugh! if you knew some of the things the girls say their fathers are at those big schools. Mind you, I don't blame them; in fact, I think it's rather nice . . ."

"Urry, what the devil? Stick to the point!"

"I think she's a Hoptroft, sir. Did you notice the resemblance? Anyhow, she calls herself Carter, and that ties up with Alf. A strong young girl like that will stick at nothing, and don't forget she doesn't come on till after eight, when the offices have been closed. Nobody would be able to say exactly if she did nip down to the coast and do a stabbing."

"You think she had it in for 'The Greek'?"

"I don't know what to think, sir, to be honest. I just don't know what to think. I only wish they'd stabbed her at Arundel or New Barnet."

Dr. Blow felt for his key. He would be glad to get safely inside his flat, and he meant to bolt the door. The encounter with Mrs. Hoptroft had greatly unsettled him. Then, as he stood hesitating at the door, a voice called through the panel, "Don't ring! I can see you!" and the light went on in the hall. Professor Manciple let him in.

"Ah, Manciple! You here? My dear fellow, it was a fruitless journey. I became separated from the young lady; I met with an extraordinary misadventure; I have been obliged to spend a great deal of money on worthless baubles—here, a great parcel of stupid silks and frills—and I was unexpectedly confronted with Mrs. Hoptroft. Make me a cup of tea, Gideon, will you? I am done up. I am all in."

"Emily will do it. Emily, my treasure, my dove, it is the Doctor! Put on a kettle, my dear. We will all take something. It has been an exhausting day."

"Manciple, Miss Emily Cakebread is most welcome in my house, you know that. But why is she here? Why are you here, for that matter? Did I inadvertently lock you in?"

"It is a long story, Blow. Sit down and take your boots off; you'll feel better. After you left this morning I felt unsettled, in no mood to wrestle with that foolish fellow Canute. His shillings were never very attractive anyway—heavy as lead and dull. Well, so I got to thinking again about dear Emily and that dreadful woman, her sister. Excuse me, Emily—ah, she did not hear. Do

183

you know, all these years Miss Cakebread has only paid her sister thirty shillings a week, and she kept back twenty-five for food and lodging. Emily had to wear all her sister's castoffs and all that."

"I suppose they had to be careful, if I was their only customer."

"I knew there was some racket. Emily was kept entirely in the dark, of course, but I have managed to piece it together. That woman had actually had a duplicate key made to your front door, Blow. She used to wander in and out practically at will. Many's the loaf and pot of jam she's made off with and little loose trifles and odd bits of money that you will leave carelessly about. But that's neither here nor there. The thing is this: she used to blackmail the housekeepers. Blackmail them, Blow! Threaten to expose them unless they left."

"Expose them, Manciple?"

"Well, she used to get a hold over them one way or another. As soon as she had a new one to send you, she used to blackmail the old one into leaving. Play on their nerves. Then, presto, around you would go and another transaction was entered on the books. All that rubbish about my second cousin being pleased with the girl Hawkins—or Harris, was it—just window dressing. They haven't had a trained servant on their books for ten years and more, Emily says."

"Then Mrs. Sollihull . . ."

"Mrs. Sollihull wasn't one to play tricks on. She had her own times and seasons for coming and going. Miss Cakebread said to her, after a couple of weeks, 'Time you went!' but Mrs. Sollihull hadn't had a chance to size up the silver. And who do you think Miss Cakebread had lined up to take her place? Miss Fisk! Think of that!"

"Look, Manciple, I can't take all this in until I drink my tea."

"And here it comes, dear fellow, here it comes—Emily, you know Dr. Blow; Dr. Blow, my fiancée—Emily and I, William, have come to an understanding."

"Dear Dr. Blow, we shall so much enjoy being neighbors!"

"Er—won't you share an establishment?"

"Neighbors of yours, she means, Blow. We shall live next door, you know. Live next door."

"Manciple, my dear fellow, forgive me, but do you think, after all these years, Mrs. Turner . . ."

"My housekeeper, Emily—Mrs. Turner—not, ha ha, in any sense some other and unsuccessful suitor, no. A woman almost entirely without ambition. Yes, Blow, why not? I can't conceive that Emily would wish to keep her on. You can cook, Emily, hey?"

"Gideon, for you I can do anything, anything."

"Just so. Yes, we will speak to Mrs. Turner. That would be a very good plan. Miss Angell is not likely to return and I can't think, Blow, that despite Miss Cakebread's very kind offer, you would wish to have her permanently in the house. It would be improper."

"Improper, Manciple? I hardly think that. Of course, I have no means of knowing what her touch might be with toasted cheese. But there could be nothing improper. Never, except in the isolated case of Mrs. Hoptroft, could there have been the slightest suspicion. Why improper, pray?"

"Improper, to employ as a housekeeper the murderer of her predecessor. Yes, Blow, Miss Cakebread murdered Flash Elsie!"

"Gideon, my dear fellow . . ."

"Not now, Blow, not now. Everything in its place. Can't you see my fiancée has fainted?"

22

"I am telephoning up to speak to Inspector Urry: URRY, Urry. He is one of the police. Yes, it is about a murder. My name is Dr. Blow. No, no, my dear man, BLOW, but there's no need to write it down. He knows me. I am not a Doctor of Medicine—I always tell them that, Manciple—I say, I am not a Doctor of Medicine. But it is irrelevant. There has not been a murder; it's the same one. You must allow me to speak, policeman! Just so. —He's gone to look for the Inspector.—Ha ha! Inspector, a little surprise for you, my dear fellow. We have got your murderer, I mean, of course, Mrs. Sollihull's murderer. You are in no danger, my dear fellow. Hey? Yes, then by all means come along. We are making tea! Good-bye."

Emily was sitting up. A disadvantage of fainting, she had noticed on previous occasions, was that one never knew what was going on when one woke. A stiff cup of tea was working wonders, aided by her lively curiosity.

They heard the door of the police car slam in the street, and the Doctor hastened into the hall. "Don't knock!" they heard him calling, "I can see you!"

"Now, what's all this?" asked the Inspector, coming in without ceremony and giving the company the barest civil nod. "I'm busy, sir. No time for idle chat. That fool Elkins said Brest, and now we've got the whole French force alerted; he calmly comes and says he's sorry, it was not Brest at all but Brest-Litovsk. I only hope Alf knows where he's going; he'll need his winter woolies."

"The arrest of Alf, Inspector, together with that of 'The Greek,' is not the more important of your preoccupations. You wish to know, do you not, who killed Mrs. Sollihull?"

"Well, never fear, sir, we shall find out."

"Yes, just so. I never doubted it. But I have felt, once or twice, that perhaps we men of learning have been able to point the way here and there. Hem, well. Yesterday you asked who killed Mrs. Sollihull and why."

"I know why now. 'She died because she wouldn't play ball,' —seems a silly reason to me, but I have it on good authority."

"I remember about the knife now," Miss Emily said suddenly. "It was the day Miss Fisk came in to ask Christina—my sister, you know—if we could get her a job. Cook-housekeeper, she asked for, though afterward she said governess; they're often snobby like that. Think it's a cut below them. But I always tell them, go where the food is. Well, I was taking down the particulars for the card and my pencil point was worn out. I couldn't just lay my hand on another and Miss Fisk suddenly pulled out this great knife and said, 'Here, try this.' So I sharpened my pencil and put the knife down, and she must have forgotten to take it with her because afterward Christina . . ."

"Afterward, Inspector, Christina left it in Mrs. Sollihull's back."

"Oh, did she, sir?"

"Yes, she did. Don't believe me if you don't want to, but just remember who told you to look in the cellar at Greek Street, and who found the knife and put you on to Miss Fisk, and the rest. Eh, Blow?"

"Certainly, Manciple. The point is well taken."

"Pray, why did Miss Cakebread do this?"

"Because—as you have graphically told us—Flash Elsie wouldn't play ball."

Emily chipped in. "You see, Inspector, it was a rule of the agency that Dr. Blow's housekeepers had to be gone within the month, and even then my sister and I were managing on little more than two hundred a year between us. But Mrs. Sollihull not only wouldn't go, she made my sister put back a jar of pickles and two chops. Christina has a dreadful temper, you know. You've heard how she sent me off like that after you came to our house.

So, without thinking-like, she took this dagger that she had with her—she'd used it to cut off the chops—and I'm very much afraid she attacked Mrs. Sollihull, you know. The blow was mortal."

"I suppose the defense will be that she didn't know her own strength!"

"She is a very passionate woman, my sister."

"I always said it was a crime of passion," Urry said, "at least that's something. All right, so you say this is what happened. Now explain this: how do you account for Mrs. Sollihull's watch. Miss Fisk came in to look for it and it wasn't there. When Dr. Blow accidentally fell across the mattress a few days later, it *was* there. *And it was ticking.*"

"You see," said Manciple patiently, "she left the knife because she knew it was Miss Fisk's—I mean, Miss Fisk had had it. It was really 'The Greek's.' Then, Miss Fisk took it away, and when Miss Cakebread knew that—the whole business was in the newspapers, you know, and there was the evidence at the inquest—then Miss Cakebread had to get something else to throw suspicion that way. She was terrified Miss Fisk would say she'd lent Miss Cakebread the knife. But if Miss Fisk were under suspicion, then anything she said would be taken as just making excuses."

"Just making excuses! For murder! Go on, sir, please."

"I say," said Dr. Blow, "all this is all very well, but what about Miss Emily destroying all those papers, hey? I know, Manciple, the lady is under your protection, but even so. . . ."

"It is necessary to establish the truth, Blow. I grant it. And so we shall. Well, Emily?"

"I was distracted, Inspector. I had no true idea what was going on. My sister was at once evasive and effusive. She talked of me having to save her, and I was her own chicken, and so on, and she never said what I had to save her from. So I did the best I could. I knew the Greek Street Agency was involved in this terrible business, and I went up there and destroyed all our correspondence with them. I thought Christina might have been fiddling the income tax. And while I was there I took the watch. It was on the desk. I'm afraid I was tempted, you know, never having had much in the way of nice things."

"Bravo," said Blow, much moved; he knew not why.

"Emily, my dear, we are assured of your innocence, so will you tell us why you were so upset when I said to you, there in the office at Greek Street, that Alf Carter's name was Cuttle?"

"Because it destroyed, for a time, my faith in the essential goodness of human nature."

"Well, that's a reasonable answer. But you say 'for a time'; what restored it?"

"Your dear love, Gideon, and the knowledge that you were mistaken and his name really *was* Carter. It's in the police records. Cuttle was the other man. But, you see, Christina had come home and said she had had a terrible scene—that's what she called it, a terrible scene—with this Mrs. Carter, Mrs. Sollihull you know. And afterward, when I heard Mrs. Carter was dead, I realized that the man I thought I loved was the widower of the woman of whom my sister was probably the murderer. My nerves were all on edge."

"I can't see how Cuttle has anything to do with this," the Inspector said mildly.

"You will, Inspector, you will," said Miss Emily, giving him a curious glance.

"One thing, at least, is certain," Urry said, looking at his watch. "I must question Miss Cakebread about all this. I suppose she's just about shutting up the shop."

"Just about," Manciple agreed.

When the Inspector had gone, Dr. Blow said, "Look here, Gideon, I'm not such an ass as you think. What exactly was all that rigmarole?"

"I'll tell you, Blow. When my little woman realized that this murder was the work of her sister, she was very cut up. She never much cared for Christina, what with being kept down and so on, but after all, murder is another matter. So she came to me and we put our heads together and we decided Urry would have to be told, because, in any case, he'd ferret it out in the end. But if we told him in our own time and in our own way, the good fellow would only half-believe it and he wouldn't rush about blowing his whistle and stirring up trouble. So we telephoned Christina and told her to clear out. Then we kept him talking, as you saw; and she's on her way by now."

"Where to?"

"We don't know," said Emily, a little tearfully.

"Better not to know, my dear. Later on, I dare say, she will send you a picture postcard. Exactly so. I remember one came one morning for Mrs. Sollihull. They like them."

"Emily, my dear," Manciple said, "where did you hire the parrot—or was it stuffed?"

"Miss Angell!"

"Yes, Dr. Blow, forgive me. It was necessary. We had no one else to send. Even Mrs. Waters was an invention. We had, literally, not a servant on our books. Not one. And we couldn't get one in time and we *couldn't* lose a customer, not when we only had one. Besides, Christina wanted to get in and hide that watch. We wound it up and left it ticking to make it easier for you."

"But all those cheese cakes, and your imaginary late first husband's alleged mother . . ."

"My sister Christina is very fond of cheese cakes."

"Well," said Dr. Blow, "I give up."

"I give up," said Inspector Urry. "We scour the streets; we comb the town; we put a cordon on the main roads and stop every car and cart and bus and wagon, even tandem bicycles and people on those potty little things with tiny wheels; and what happens?"

"What happens?" asked the Chief Constable. He knew, but he felt that if Inspector Urry didn't get the thing off his chest he'd burst.

"We put Abner on the beach, where he can do the least harm, and he sees a lady in a brand-new yellow cape still marked 'Ideal for Gardening, Eighteen and eleven,' and he says to her, 'Madam,' he says, 'where might you be going?'

" 'I'm going a-fishing,' says she, 'help me to push out my hubby's boat.'

"So he ups along the jetty and he starts up the engine of the finest and fastest cabin cruiser in the harbor for her. 'And who might your husband be?' he asks, checking up on her in the course of duty. 'He's the Suffragan Bishop,' she says, very sweet. So he lets her go."

"At least Abner's consistent," said the Chief Constable.

THE PERENNIAL LIBRARY MYSTERY SERIES

Delano Ames

CORPSE DIPLOMATIQUE   P 637, $2.84
"Sprightly and intelligent."
                                            —*New York Herald Tribune Book Review*

FOR OLD CRIME'S SAKE   P 629, $2.84

MURDER, MAESTRO, PLEASE   P 630, $2.84
"If there is a more engaging couple in modern fiction than Jane and
Dagobert Brown, we have not met them."   —*Scotsman*

SHE SHALL HAVE MURDER   P 638, $2.84
"Combines the merit of both the English and American schools in the
new mystery. It's as breezy as the best of the American ones, and has
the sophistication and wit of any top-notch Britisher."
                                            —*New York Herald Tribune Book Review*

E. C. Bentley

TRENT'S LAST CASE   P 440, $2.50
"One of the three best detective stories ever written."
                                            —Agatha Christie

TRENT'S OWN CASE   P 516, $2.25
"I won't waste time saying that the plot is sound and the detection
satisfying. Trent has not altered a scrap and reappears with all his old
humor and charm."   —Dorothy L. Sayers

Gavin Black

A DRAGON FOR CHRISTMAS   P 473, $1.95
"Potent excitement!"   —*New York Herald Tribune*

THE EYES AROUND ME   P 485, $1.95
"I stayed up until all hours last night reading *The Eyes Around Me,*
which is something I do not do very often, but I was so intrigued by the
ingeniousness of Mr. Black's plotting and the witty way in which he spins
his mystery. I can only say that I enjoyed the book enormously."
                                            —F. van Wyck Mason

YOU WANT TO DIE, JOHNNY?   P 472, $1.95
"Gavin Black doesn't just develop a pressure plot in suspense, he adds
uninfected wit, character, charm, and sharp knowledge of the Far East
to make rereading as keen as the first race-through."   —*Book Week*

Nicholas Blake

THE CORPSE IN THE SNOWMAN P 427, $1.95

"If there is a distinction between the novel and the detective story (which we do not admit), then this book deserves a high place in both categories." —*The New York Times*

THE DREADFUL HOLLOW P 493, $1.95

"Pace unhurried, characters excellent, reasoning solid."

—*San Francisco Chronicle*

END OF CHAPTER P 397, $1.95

". . . admirably solid . . . an adroit formal detective puzzle backed up by firm characterization and a knowing picture of London publishing."

—*The New York Times*

HEAD OF A TRAVELER P 398, $2.25

"Another grade A detective story of the right old jigsaw persuasion."

—*New York Herald Tribune Book Review*

MINUTE FOR MURDER P 419, $1.95

"An outstanding mystery novel. Mr. Blake's writing is a delight in itself." —*The New York Times*

THE MORNING AFTER DEATH P 520, $1.95

"One of Blake's best." —Rex Warner

A PENKNIFE IN MY HEART P 521, $2.25

"Style brilliant . . . and suspenseful." —*San Francisco Chronicle*

THE PRIVATE WOUND P 531, $2.25

[Blake's] best novel in a dozen years . . . . An intensely penetrating study of sexual passion. . . . A powerful story of murder and its aftermath."

—Anthony Boucher, *The New York Times*

A QUESTION OF PROOF P 494, $1.95

"The characters in this story are unusually well drawn, and the suspense is well sustained." —*The New York Times*

THE SAD VARIETY P 495, $2.25

"It is a stunner. I read it instead of eating, instead of sleeping."

—Dorothy Salisbury Davis

THERE'S TROUBLE BREWING P 569, $3.37

"Nigel Strangeways is a puzzling mixture of simplicity and penetration, but all the more real for that." —*The Times Literary Supplement*

Nicholas Blake (cont'd)

THOU SHELL OF DEATH   P 428, $1.95
"It has all the virtues of culture, intelligence and sensibility that the most exacting connoisseur could ask of detective fiction."
                    —*The Times* [London] *Literary Supplement*

THE WIDOW'S CRUISE   P 399, $2.25
"A stirring suspense. . . . The thrilling tale leaves nothing to be desired."
                    —*Springfield Republican*

THE WORM OF DEATH   P 400, $2.25
"It [The Worm of Death] is one of Blake's very best—and his best is better than almost anyone's."   —Louis Untermeyer

John & Emery Bonett

A BANNER FOR PEGASUS   P 554, $2.40
"A gem! Beautifully plotted and set. . . . Not only is the murder adroit and deserved, and the detection competent, but the love story is charming."   —Jacques Barzun and Wendell Hertig Taylor

DEAD LION   P 563, $2.40
"A clever plot, authentic background and interesting characters highly recommended this one."   —*New Republic*

Christianna Brand

GREEN FOR DANGER   P 551, $2.50
"You have to reach for the greatest of Great Names (Christie, Carr, Queen . . .) to find Brand's rivals in the devious subtleties of the trade."
                    —Anthony Boucher

TOUR DE FORCE   P 572, $2.40
"Complete with traps for the over-ingenious, a double-reverse surprise ending and a key clue planted so fairly and obviously that you completely overlook it. If that's your idea of perfect entertainment, then seize at once upon *Tour de Force.*"   —Anthony Boucher, *The New York Times*

James Byrom

OR BE HE DEAD   P 585, $2.84
"A very original tale . . . Well written and steadily entertaining."
    —Jacques Barzun & Wendell Hertig Taylor, *A Catalogue of Crime*

Henry Calvin

IT'S DIFFERENT ABROAD   P 640, $2.84

"What is remarkable and delightful, Mr. Calvin imparts a flavor of satire
to what he renovates and compels us to take straight."

—Jacques Barzun

Marjorie Carleton

VANISHED   P 559, $2.40

"Exceptional . . . a minor triumph."

—Jacques Barzun and Wendell Hertig Taylor, *A Catalogue of Crime*

George Harmon Coxe

MURDER WITH PICTURES   P 527, $2.25

"[Coxe] has hit the bull's-eye with his first shot."

—*The New York Times*

Edmund Crispin

BURIED FOR PLEASURE   P 506, $2.50

"Absolute and unalloyed delight."

—Anthony Boucher, *The New York Times*

Lionel Davidson

THE MENORAH MEN   P 592, $2.84

"Of his fellow thriller writers, only John Le Carré shows the same
instinct for the viscera."   —*Chicago Tribune*

NIGHT OF WENCESLAS   P 595, $2.84

"A most ingenious thriller, so enriched with style, wit, and a sense of
serious comedy that it all but transcends its kind."

—*The New Yorker*

THE ROSE OF TIBET   P 593, $2.84

"I hadn't realized how much I missed the genuine Adventure story
. . . until I read *The Rose of Tibet*."   —Graham Greene

D. M. Devine

MY BROTHER'S KILLER   P 558, $2.40

"A most enjoyable crime story which I enjoyed reading down to the last
moment."   —Agatha Christie

Kenneth Fearing

THE BIG CLOCK   P 500, $1.95
"It will be some time before chill-hungry clients meet again so rare a compound of irony, satire, and icy-fingered narrative. *The Big Clock* is . . . a psychothriller you won't put down."   —*Weekly Book Review*

Andrew Garve

THE ASHES OF LODA   P 430, $1.50
"Garve . . . embellishes a fine fast adventure story with a more credible picture of the U.S.S.R. than is offered in most thrillers."
                                        —*The New York Times Book Review*

THE CUCKOO LINE AFFAIR   P 451, $1.95
". . . an agreeable and ingenious piece of work."   —*The New Yorker*

A HERO FOR LEANDA   P 429, $1.50
"One can trust Mr. Garve to put a fresh twist to any situation, and the ending is really a lovely surprise."   —*The Manchester Guardian*

MURDER THROUGH THE LOOKING GLASS   P 449, $1.95
". . . refreshingly out-of-the-way and enjoyable . . . highly recommended to all comers."   —*Saturday Review*

NO TEARS FOR HILDA   P 441, $1.95
"It starts fine and finishes finer. I got behind on breathing watching Max get not only his man but his woman, too."   —Rex Stout

THE RIDDLE OF SAMSON   P 450, $1.95
"The story is an excellent one, the people are quite likable, and the writing is superior."   —*Springfield Republican*

Michael Gilbert

BLOOD AND JUDGMENT   P 446, $1.95
"Gilbert readers need scarcely be told that the characters all come alive at first sight, and that his surpassing talent for narration enhances any plot. . . . Don't miss."   —*San Francisco Chronicle*

THE BODY OF A GIRL   P 459, $1.95
"Does what a good mystery should do: open up into all kinds of ramifications, with untold menace behind the action. At the end, there is a bang-up climax, and it is a pleasure to see how skilfully Gilbert wraps everything up."   —*The New York Times Book Review*

Michael Gilbert (cont'd)

THE DANGER WITHIN   P 448, $1.95
"Michael Gilbert has nicely combined some elements of the straight detective story with plenty of action, suspense, and adventure, to produce a superior thriller."   *—Saturday Review*

FEAR TO TREAD   P 458, $1.95
"Merits serious consideration as a work of art."

                                    —The New York Times

Joe Gores

HAMMETT   P 631, $2.84
"Joe Gores at his very best. Terse, powerful writing—with the master, Dashiell Hammett, as the protagonist in a novel I think he would have been proud to call his own."   *—Robert Ludlum*

C. W. Grafton

BEYOND A REASONABLE DOUBT   P 519, $1.95
"A very ingenious tale of murder . . . a brilliant and gripping narrative."
                —Jacques Barzun and Wendell Hertig Taylor

THE RAT BEGAN TO GNAW THE ROPE   P 639, $2.84
"Fast, humorous story with flashes of brilliance."

                                    —The New Yorker

Edward Grierson

THE SECOND MAN   P 528, $2.25
"One of the best trial-testimony books to have come along in quite a while."   *—The New Yorker*

Bruce Hamilton

TOO MUCH OF WATER   P 635, $2.84
"A superb sea mystery. . . . The prose is excellent."
  —Jacques Barzun and Wendell Hertig Taylor, A Catalogue of Crime

Cyril Hare

DEATH IS NO SPORTSMAN   P 555, $2.40
"You will be thrilled because it succeeds in placing an ingenious story in a new and refreshing setting. . . . The identity of the murderer is really a surprise."   *—Daily Mirror*

DEATH WALKS THE WOODS   P 556, $2.40

"Here is a fine formal detective story, with a technically brilliant solution demanding the attention of all connoisseurs of construction."

—Anthony Boucher, *The New York Times Book Review*

AN ENGLISH MURDER   P 455, $2.50

"By a long shot, the best crime story I have read for a long time. Everything is traditional, but originality does not suffer. The setting is perfect. Full marks to Mr. Hare."   —*Irish Press*

SUICIDE EXCEPTED   P 636, $2.84

"Adroit in its manipulation . . . and distinguished by a plot-twister which I'll wager Christie wishes she'd thought of."

—*The New York Times*

TENANT FOR DEATH   P 570, $2.84

"The way in which an air of probability is combined both with clear, terse narrative and with a good deal of subtle suburban atmosphere, proves the extreme skill of the writer."   —*The Spectator*

TRAGEDY AT LAW   P 522, $2.25

"An extremely urbane and well-written detective story."

—*The New York Times*

UNTIMELY DEATH   P 514, $2.25

"The English detective story at its quiet best, meticulously underplayed, rich in perceivings of the droll human animal and ready at the last with a neat surprise which has been there all the while had we but wits to see it."   —*New York Herald Tribune Book Review*

THE WIND BLOWS DEATH   P 589, $2.84

"A plot compounded of musical knowledge, a Dickens allusion, and a subtle point in law is related with delightfully unobtrusive wit, warmth, and style."   —*The New York Times*

WITH A BARE BODKIN   P 523, $2.25

"One of the best detective stories published for a long time."

—*The Spectator*

Robert Harling

THE ENORMOUS SHADOW   P 545, $2.50

"In some ways the best spy story of the modern period. . . . The writing is terse and vivid . . . the ending full of action . . . altogether first-rate."

—Jacques Barzun and Wendell Hertig Taylor, *A Catalogue of Crime*

Matthew Head

THE CABINDA AFFAIR   P 541, $2.25
"An absorbing whodunit and a distinguished novel of atmosphere."
                              —Anthony Boucher, *The New York Times*

THE CONGO VENUS   P 597, $2.84
"Terrific. The dialogue is just plain wonderful."
                                          —*The Boston Globe*

MURDER AT THE FLEA CLUB   P 542, $2.50
"The true delight is in Head's style, its limpid ease combined with humor
and an awesome precision of phrase."   —*San Francisco Chronicle*

M. V. Heberden

ENGAGED TO MURDER   P 533, $2.25
"Smooth plotting."   —*The New York Times*

James Hilton

WAS IT MURDER?   P 501, $1.95
"The story is well planned and well written."
                                          —*The New York Times*

P. M. Hubbard

HIGH TIDE   P 571, $2.40
"A smooth elaboration of mounting horror and danger."
                                          —*Library Journal*

Elspeth Huxley

THE AFRICAN POISON MURDERS   P 540, $2.25
"Obscure venom, manical mutilations, deadly bush fire, thrilling climax
compose major opus.... Top-flight."
                                  —*Saturday Review of Literature*

MURDER ON SAFARI   P 587, $2.84
"Right now we'd call Mrs. Huxley a dangerous rival to Agatha Christie."   —*Books*

Mary Kelly

THE SPOILT KILL   P 565, $2.40

"Mary Kelly is a new Dorothy Sayers. . . . [An] exciting new novel."
                                        —*Evening News*

Lange Lewis

THE BIRTHDAY MURDER   P 518, $1.95

"Almost perfect in its playlike purity and delightful prose."
                        —Jacques Barzun and Wendell Hertig Taylor

Allan MacKinnon

HOUSE OF DARKNESS   P 582, $2.84

"His best . . . a perfect compendium."
   —Jacques Barzun & Wendell Hertig Taylor, *A Catalogue of Crime*

Arthur Maling

LUCKY DEVIL   P 482, $1.95

"The plot unravels at a fast clip, the writing is breezy and Maling's
approach is as fresh as today's stockmarket quotes."
                                —*Louisville Courier Journal*

RIPOFF   P 483, $1.95

"A swiftly paced story of today's big business is larded with intrigue as
a Ralph Nader-type investigates an insurance scandal and is soon on the
run from a hired gun and his brother. . . . Engrossing and credible."
                                        —*Booklist*

SCHROEDER'S GAME   P 484, $1.95

"As the title indicates, this Schroeder is up to something, and the un-
ravelling of his game is a diverting and sufficiently blood-soaked entertainment."   —*The New Yorker*

Austin Ripley

MINUTE MYSTERIES   P 387, $2.50

More than one hundred of the world's shortest detective stories. Only
one possible solution to each case!

Thomas Sterling

THE EVIL OF THE DAY   P 529, $2.50

"Prose as witty and subtle as it is sharp and clear. . .characters unconven-
tionally conceived and richly bodied forth . . . . In short, a novel to be
treasured."   —Anthony Boucher, *The New York Times*

Julian Symons

THE BELTING INHERITANCE P 468, $1.95
"A superb whodunit in the best tradition of the detective story."
—August Derleth, *Madison Capital Times*

BLAND BEGINNING P 469, $1.95
"Mr. Symons displays a deft storytelling skill, a quiet and literate wit, a nice feeling for character, and detectival ingenuity of a high order."
—Anthony Boucher, *The New York Times*

BOGUE'S FÓRTUNE P 481, $1.95
"There's a touch of the old sardonic humour, and more than a touch of style." —*The Spectator*

THE BROKEN PENNY P 480, $1.95
"The most exciting, astonishing and believable spy story to appear in years. —Anthony Boucher, *The New York Times Book Review*

THE COLOR OF MURDER P 461, $1.95
"A singularly unostentatious and memorably brilliant detective story."
—*New York Herald Tribune Book Review*

Dorothy Stockbridge Tillet
(John Stephen Strange)

THE MAN WHO KILLED FORTESCUE P 536, $2.25
"Better than average." —*Saturday Review of Literature*

Simon Troy

THE ROAD TO RHUINE P 583, $2.84
"Unusual and agreeably told." —*San Francisco Chronicle*

SWIFT TO ITS CLOSE P 546, $2.40
"A nicely literate British mystery . . . the atmosphere and the plot are exceptionally well wrought, the dialogue excellent." —*Best Sellers*

Henry Wade

THE DUKE OF YORK'S STEPS P 588, $2.84
"A classic of the golden age."
—Jacques Barzun & Wendell Hertig Taylor, *A Catalogue of Crime*

A DYING FALL P 543, $2.50
"One of those expert British suspense jobs . . . it crackles with undercurrents of blackmail, violent passion and murder. Topnotch in its class."
—*Time*

Henry Wade (cont'd)

THE HANGING CAPTAIN   P 548, $2.50
"This is a detective story for connoisseurs, for those who value clear
thinking and good writing above mere ingenuity and easy thrills."
                                   —*Times Literary Supplement*

Hillary Waugh

LAST SEEN WEARING . . .   P 552, $2.40
"A brilliant tour de force."   —Julian Symons

THE MISSING MAN   P 553, $2.40
"The quiet detailed police work of Chief Fred C. Fellows, Stockford,
Conn., is at its best in *The Missing Man* . . . one of the Chief's toughest
cases and one of the best handled."
            —Anthony Boucher, *The New York Times Book Review*

Henry Kitchell Webster

WHO IS THE NEXT?   P 539, $2.25
"A double murder, private-plane piloting, a neat impersonation, and a
delicate courtship are adroitly combined by a writer who knows how to
use the language."   —Jacques Barzun and Wendell Hertig Taylor

Anna Mary Wells

MURDERER'S CHOICE   P 534, $2.50
"Good writing, ample action, and excellent character work."
                                   —*Saturday Review of Literature*

A TALENT FOR MURDER   P 535, $2.25
"The discovery of the villain is a decided shock."   —*Books*

Edward Young

THE FIFTH PASSENGER   P 544, $2.25
"Clever and adroit . . . excellent thriller . . ."   —*Library Journal*

If you enjoyed this book you'll want to know about
THE PERENNIAL LIBRARY MYSTERY SERIES

Buy them at your local bookstore or use this coupon for ordering:

Qty	P number	Price
_____	_____	_____
_____	_____	_____
_____	_____	_____
_____	_____	_____
_____	_____	_____
_____	_____	_____
_____	_____	_____
_____	_____	_____
_____	_____	_____
_____	_____	_____
_____	_____	_____
_____	_____	_____
_____	_____	_____
_____	_____	_____
_____	postage and handling charge	$1.00
	_____ book(s) @ $0.25	_____
	TOTAL